Chance

in

Helen

D1483974

Books by Susan McBride

Not a Chance in Helen

A RIVER ROAD MYSTERY

SUSAN McBRIDE

WITNESS
IMPULSE

An Imprint of HarperCollinsPublishers

Recipe for *Susan McBride's (Mostly) Healthy Tomato-Pesto Grilled Cheese* copyright © 2014 by Susan McBride.

Excerpt from *Say Yes to the Death* copyright © 2015 by Susan McBride.

EPub Edition September 2014 ISBN: 9780062359797
Print Edition ISBN: 9780062359810

10 9 8 7 6 5 4 3 2 1

Prologue

THE CAB PULLED up in front of the turreted Victorian mansion, and Eleanora Duncan emerged from the backseat. She plucked cash from her wallet to press through the opened window. The driver snatched away the bills and the taxi rolled off, leaving her standing in a cloud of exhaust fumes.

She coughed, waving a gloved hand before her, thinking that between good old pollution and the cigar-smoking board members at the committee meetings she was forever attending, her poor lungs wouldn't last to blow out eighty-one candles on her birthday cake.

She hobbled up the porch steps, pulling off her gloves and stuffing them into her purse. As she reached the front door, she found it ajar.

Heavens to Betsy! She'd only been away for an hour to take her seat on the county hospital board. Had Zelma lost her mind? Eleanora could hardly believe her long-time housekeeper would leave the house accessible to any common thief.

Or worse still, she mused, what if the cat had gotten out?

As if on cue, Lady Godiva's whiskered face peered around the jamb. Before Eleanora could shove the cat back inside, the feline slipped through the door. She brushed past Eleanora's ankles and took off without a moment's hesitation.

"Lady!" Eleanora called to her precious baby. "Sweetheart, come back here this minute!" She frowned, watching her prized Persian scoot down the porch steps toward the street.

"Bad girl!" Eleanora scolded in a voice two octaves higher than normal. "You know you're not allowed to roam the neighborhood." She pressed blue-veined hands together, thinking of the things her baby could pick up outdoors: the ticks, the fleas, a dirty tom's wanton interest.

"Zelma!" she hollered as she hurried through the door and ducked her head into the foyer. "Zelma? Where the devil are you?"

Damned if the woman wasn't deaf as well as blind, she thought of the housekeeper who'd been with her longer than her husband and son, both of whom had passed two years before, God rest their souls.

Well, Eleanora couldn't wait for Zelma to appear. She turned around in the doorframe and caught sight of Lady Godiva there on the cobblestone path, sniffing at the bordering begonias. "Lady!" she called out again and hooked her purse on the doorknob. Her low heels tapped on the porch floor as she made her way after the cat, her arthritic hips slowing her gait.

She was but a few yards away when the copper-hued Persian lifted her head, tail twitching. Eleanora reached out her arms, smiling hesitantly.

"Come here, precious. Come to Mommy."

She was almost near enough to bend and scoop up Lady when a butterfly swooped down from the sky, fluttering enticingly, and the cat plunged off the curb and into the road.

"Lady Godiva, no!" Eleanora frantically scanned the street right and left, sighing when she saw no traffic. "Please, come back, pretty girl. Oh, for Pete's sake."

By then, she was breathing hard, her silk blouse uncomfortably warm against her skin. She pressed her palm to the rough bark of an oak tree and leaned against it.

Up the block, a car engine coughed to life, but Eleanora ignored it. Her attention was solely on Lady, who'd stopped to clean herself right there in the middle of the gravel-strewn road.

"Eleanora, hello there!" a familiar voice called out.

Eleanora momentarily shifted her gaze away from Lady to see a sweat-suited Helen Evans walking toward her up the sidewalk. But she neither answered nor waved.

Instead, she took in a deep breath and stepped into the street.

The squeal of tires filled her ears, and she froze like a deer caught in headlights as a car came out of nowhere and bore down on her.

"Eleanora!"

A hand snatched at her, dragging her from harm's way just as the car screeched past, kicking up so much gravel and dust in its wake that it seemed to disappear in a puff of smoke like a magician's grand finale.

She clung to her rescuer, her heart pounding in her ears and pumping the blood far too quickly through her veins. Eleanora shuddered, looking up into the gently lined face framed by gray.

"Oh, God, Helen," she got out despite the dryness of her mouth, clinging to the woman's arms for strength. "I think somebody's trying to kill me."

"I'm sorry. I was looking for my friend Jean, but I must've stumbled into Julia Child's kitchen by mistake."

"Oh, Helen, stop it." Jean Duncan blushed and threw up a hand as if to dismiss the thinly veiled compliment. "I'm just trying out a few things, experimenting, if you will."

"Pretty good-smelling experiments," Helen said and closed the screen door behind her. She entered the room with her nose lifted to inhale the mingling of scents, and she leaned her hands against the stretch of countertop to survey the goings-on. Stainless steel bowls, measuring cups, and wooden cutting boards littered with the finely chopped remains of onions and chives filled every inch of space. Several copper pots topped the burners on the stove, their contents softly gurgling.

Helen glanced around and caught sight of herself in the smoky glass of the built-in refrigerator. Sometimes it still surprised her to see a seventy-five-year-old woman in her reflection, albeit not a bad-looking one. Half the time she expected to see the dark-haired beauty she'd been in her youth, the energetic girl who'd graduated from Washington University when it still hadn't been fashionable to do so, who'd married at twenty-one and raised four children, all married with children themselves.

She touched a hand to her unruly hair but dropped it again as the click of the oven door disrupted her thoughts. She turned to Jean. "It looks like the Cordon Bleu around here," she remarked and sniffed. "Is that shrimp . . . oh, my, and Roquefort?"

Jean lifted the lid off a pot, allowing a cloud of steam to sneak out, wilting wisps of silver against her brow. "Right on both counts," she said. "Shrimp for the stuffed mushrooms and Roquefort for the chilled spinach dish." She settled the lid on the pot and gestured around her with a wooden spoon. "And, of course, there are onions and herbs for the liver pâté."

"Special occasion?"

"As a matter of fact, yes, very special." Jean snatched up a mixing bowl and hugged it to her belly, stirring its contents as she spoke. "I've finally decided to go for it."

"Go for what?" Helen tensed. At her age, that could mean anything from buying a Miracle Ear to selling the house and moving into Shady Acres.

Jean's smile widened. "The catering business I've talked about starting ever since"—she hesitated but quickly picked up where she'd left off—"ever since Jim died. Well, I've been moping around for two years, and this morning

I woke up and decided to get on with my life, doing what I do best." She lifted her chin. "And that happens to be cooking for other people."

"That's marvelous," Helen told her, feeling as thrilled by the announcement as Jean did. Her friend looked good, better than she had in a long while. After the tragic car accident that had taken Jim's life, Jean had put on weight, until she'd seemed a sad, bloated version of the lively woman Helen had remembered. Now, the sixty-year-old widow was back to her fighting form, trim and full of energy in her tan slacks and yellow sweater overlapped by a white apron. A bright scarf drew her hair off her shoulders and into a ponytail. The smile on her mouth lit up her round face, giving it a rosy glow. Her hazel eyes looked bright, which cheered Helen to no end, as there'd been too many days when they'd filled with tears at the drop of a hat.

" . . . so that suits it, don't you think?"

Helen blinked, knowing she'd missed something. "I'm sorry, what did you say?"

"Just that I'm calling it The Catery," Jean replied, talking over her shoulder as she added eggs then onions to the goose liver. "You like it? Or is it, I don't know, too simple?"

"I've always liked simple."

"Good. Because I've already had some little deli containers made up with the name. I thought I'd get a few samples around, you know, to the Ladies Civic Improvement League and such."

"Speaking of the LCIL," Helen said, an idea cooking in her brain. "The annual luncheon's just about a month away and I don't believe anyone's been hired to do the food yet."

"No, they haven't. I checked," Jean remarked and tapped a spoon in the air. "But wait'll I show them what I've got in mind," she said and grinned. Then she fixed her attention on the ingredients to her pâté de foie gras.

"Well, you've got my vote anyway," Helen told her. "The glop they served last year tasted like it was catered by the bait shop."

"Oh, Helen!"

"Well, it's true," she said, tapping a finger to her chin as another idea popped up. "The LCIL has a board meeting in the morning. It could help your cause if you showed up with some of your goodies."

"That's perfect." Jean's eyes widened. "Any suggestions?"

"It all looks good," Helen admitted, reaching over a colander filled with huge mushrooms to snatch a cheese puff from a batch not long out of the oven. She popped it into her mouth, chewing slowly, her eyes closing as she bit into the olive at the center. Was that paprika, she wondered, feeling her mouth tingle a bit, her cheeks flush. And cayenne pepper? She swallowed reluctantly and sighed aloud. When she opened her eyes, she found Jean watching her.

"Do I pass muster?" Jean asked, crossing her arms under her breasts. "Or should I quit now before I've started?"

Helen finished licking the tips of her fingers. Then she brushed her hands together, eyeing the rest of the cheese balls. "My dear, I think you've found your calling."

Jean laughed. "I'll be the Mother Teresa of the card

party set. Just give me a hungry bridge player, and I'll save her from starvation with a bowl of artichoke dip."

"Speaking of mothers," Helen began, wondering if now was the best time to broach the subject of Eleanora Duncan, what with Jean in such a good mood and all. But she swallowed any hesitation and plunged ahead. "I saw your former mother-in-law earlier when I was out for a walk, and she was . . . "

"Oh, I can only imagine what she was doing," Jean said, cutting her off. Her face tensed and the smile left her mouth, replaced by tight lips. "Knowing her, she was probably stealing candy from babies."

"Jean," Helen softly chided, but she couldn't blame Jean for her anger. Eleanora Duncan had as good as branded Jean a murderer after Jim had died, and all because Jean had been at the wheel that rainy night of the accident. The feud that Eleanora had provoked with Jean made the one between the Hatfields and McCoys look like mere bickering in comparison.

Hardly a one of the two hundred inhabitants of tiny River Bend, Illinois, hadn't been a witness to Eleanora's lingering bitterness toward Jean. Having an eighty-year-old woman call her sixty-year-old daughter-in-law "Lucrezia Borgia" in the cereal aisle at the corner market wasn't something one easily forgot. But that wasn't the worst of it. Eleanora had made headlines when she'd used her considerable influence, the type only old money can buy, to push for a coroner's inquest of Jim's death. As expected, nothing had come of it except greater animosity between Eleanora and Jean.

Helen went around the island to where Jean leaned over the counter, furiously whisking a pair of eggs to their frothy deaths.

She touched her arm, and Jean let out a cry of pain. Helen took the bowl and whisk from her and set them aside. Then she picked up Jean's hands and held them tightly. "She's an old woman who wanted someone to blame, and you happened to be it."

Tears welled in Jean's eyes though she blinked mightily, clearly determined not to cry. "She put me through hell, you know she did, as if what happened to Jim weren't enough. I felt guilty enough without her adding to it."

"Someone nearly ran her over this morning," Helen said without further dillydallying.

Jean stared at her. "What?"

"I saw Eleanora step off the curb just as a car pulled into the street and almost hit her. It would have if I hadn't gotten to her first," Helen added.

"Maybe the driver didn't see her."

Helen shook her head. "The car sped up and never slowed down. It felt very deliberate."

"Oh." Jean paled, looking suddenly shaky. Helen guided her away from the mixing bowls and boiling shrimp and chopped onions, setting her down at the breakfast table. "Oh, my goodness," she continued, her voice falling to a whisper. "Was she hit?"

"Not even scratched."

Jean wet her lips. "Did you recognize who was at the wheel?"

"It all happened so fast." Helen sighed, letting go of

Jean's hands to pluck at several tufts of cat hair stuck to the legs of her pants. Amber's telltale yellow fur. She'd have to start brushing him now that spring had come, no matter how the old tom resisted.

"Is she okay?"

Helen glanced up, and her eyes met Jean's again. "As you'd expect, Eleanora was quite shaken."

Jean murmured, "The poor dear."

Within a few minutes, Eleanora Duncan had gone from being accused of stealing lollipops from babies to being "the poor dear." Helen smiled despite herself, thinking the scare Eleanora had had this morning might actually result in something positive after all.

"Maybe I should"—Jean started to say but hesitated, squinting into the distance—"well, I'm probably the last person Eleanora wants to see, and I can't say I feel any differently about her. But, like you said, Helen, she's had to deal with losing a husband and son while she continues to live and breathe. I know she doesn't have many close friends despite all those committees she sits on. She's really all alone. Aw, hell," Jean groaned and let her head roll back. "I may be a fool, but I think I'll go by her place later on and take her something to eat. A little liver pâté, maybe some crab dip and stuffed mushrooms. What do you think?"

Helen stood and patted Jean's shoulder. "Sounds like a grand idea. With the way you cook, it might do a lot toward mending fences."

Jean got up as well and wiped her hands on her apron, nodding as if to convince herself it might possibly be true.

She walked Helen out, holding the screen door wide open with her hip. "Just so long as she doesn't accuse me of trying to poison her," she remarked before she waved Helen off.

"That's the spirit!" Helen laughed as she headed down the driveway toward the sidewalk.

Chapter 2

"WELL, THERE YOU are, for heaven's sake. Just where have you been all this time?"

Zelma Burdine set down the shopping bag on the kitchen counter with a thump. Then she removed the scarf that bound her thin brown hair and stuffed it in her coat pocket. "I had to go into Alton, Miss Nora, just like I told you yesterday."

Eleanora took a step further into the kitchen. She'd exchanged the uncomfortable pumps for a pair of cushioned flats. The soles squished audibly as she crossed the room. "Do you realize you left the front door wide open?"

Her coat half off, Zelma paused and looked over at Eleanora. Her tiny eyes looked even smaller as she stared through Coke bottle-thick glasses. "I did what?"

"The front door," Eleanora repeated huffily. "You didn't shut it properly, much less lock it. If I hadn't arrived home when I did, who knows what might have happened to

Lady Godiva." When she finished, Eleanora felt herself get steamed up all over again.

Zelma shrugged off her coat entirely and hung it on one of the hooks near the back door. "Did the cat get out?" she asked timidly, her voice so small that it was a wonder Eleanora even heard.

But Eleanora's ears were as sharp as a bat's. They were the one part of her body that hadn't failed her yet.

"Of course she got out, you ninny!" she shrilled. "My baby slipped right past me and into the street. She could have been killed! I was very nearly killed myself when I went after her."

"You were nearly killed, ma'am?" Zelma turned around, hands clasped at her thin bosom. Her eyes went wide behind the thick lenses.

Eleanora jerked her chin up and down. "I came an inch from being run over."

"Jesus, Joseph, and Mary," Zelma breathed, her pinched features looking a tinge on the green side. "You weren't hurt?"

"Well, I'm standing here, aren't I?"

Zelma nodded, mouth compressed.

"If I had been flattened, it would have been your fault, wouldn't it? You'd be to blame," Eleanora blurted out, unable to hold her tongue. Why, Zelma was a good ten years younger than she and was supposed to do the taking care of around here. At moments like this, however, Eleanora felt as if she was the nursemaid and Zelma the one who needed looking after.

Oh, how she'd been tempted to get rid of the old girl

time and again, but what would Zelma do without her? If not for this job, she'd have only Social Security to live on and not a stitch of family to check up on her. She had no one but Eleanora, who, after all these years, was about as near to a blood tie as Zelma would get. Yes, if she canned her, what person in her right mind would hire Zelma Burdine? The fool was losing her hearing and could hardly see two feet before her. It was a wonder the Department of Motor Vehicles hadn't pulled her driver's license already, which was one reason Eleanora was forever taking taxis. She was too afraid to let Zelma drive her anywhere.

"I'm glad you're all right, ma'am," Zelma whispered.

"I'm sure you are," Eleanora said, though Zelma's remark had taken some of the piss and vinegar out of her. "Did you deliver those papers to my lawyers, like I asked?"

"Yes, ma'am." Her housekeeper nodded. "I handed them to the secretary myself."

"Good girl."

Zelma nodded and stepped up to the counter. She removed some containers from the brown paper sack and put them in the refrigerator.

Eleanora peered over her shoulder. "Is that the food Lady likes so much?"

Zelma finished placing the containers in the fridge then straightened. "It is," she said and pressed a finger to the bridge of her glasses. "From that fancy boutique store that makes all their grub from scratch. Though I don't know for the life of me why she can't eat the regular store-bought stuff. Other cats do," she murmured as she closed the refrigerator and folded up the emptied sack.

Eleanora's hand went to her heart. "I'll pretend I didn't hear that."

Though Zelma continued to mutter, "I don't see why you spoil her so much, acting like she's a child. She's just a cat."

Eleanora bristled. She stared at Zelma, at the owlish face topped by sparse tufts of hair, at the stoop of her back, feeling as if she was looking at a stranger. "Lady," she hissed, "is hardly 'just' a cat."

"So it seems."

"And see that you don't forget it!"

Zelma tied on her apron, sighing quietly. "How could I?"

Hearing Zelma's dispirited tone of voice and seeing the sag of her shoulders tugged at something in Eleanora. She shuffled up beside her and cupped swollen fingers beneath the housekeeper's chin.

"Dear Zelma," she said and peered at the wizened features, thinking that neither of them had aged particularly well. But they were both alive, weren't they? Both walking on two legs and breathing without any appliances attached. "We've been through a lot together, haven't we?" She smiled and patted Zelma's wrinkled cheek. "You were with me when I first married, when Marvin and I built up the business, and when my son was born." She swallowed and braced herself for the words to follow, ones much harder to say. "And you stood by me as well when Marvin had his heart attack and when I lost my darling Jim. What would I have done without you?" she asked, forgetting that moments ago she'd been envisioning just that. "What would we do without each other?"

Zelma's eyes brightened. Her cheeks flushed, and Eleanora was afraid she'd embarrassed the old girl.

"Ah, well, I've things to do," she said and let her hand drop. She left Zelma standing at the sink to take care of the dishes. "I'll be in the library should you need me."

"Yes, ma'am."

Eleanor crossed the wood-planked hallway with its worn Turkish rugs, bypassing the antiques-filled living room and the dining room with its Chippendale table and chairs, heading for the door at the far end.

Lady was there waiting for her. Perched atop the cushion of a Louis XV chair, the Persian raised her head as Eleanora entered. Her pug features appeared to be grinning. Eleanora went to her and rubbed the soft fur until Lady purred like a well-oiled engine. Eleanora clucked and cooed for another few minutes before she let the cat alone and took her seat behind the English writing desk.

Invitations sat in a neat little pile in the middle of her blotter. Requests for donations to this charity or that were stacked in another. She sighed and leaned back in the plump wing chair that had once been Marvin's and still smelled of his pipe tobacco.

Was there anyone except Zelma who didn't want something from her, either her time or her money or both?

Ah, to be old and rich, she mused, knowing the combination often brought more angst than pleasure.

A face popped into her head, dark eyes topped by severely plucked brows, high cheekbones that carved furrows into cheeks.

Ugh, Eleanora thought and pressed her fingers to her temples, as if the mere motion could wipe away the image.

Jemima Winthrop.

The name alone made her grind her teeth.

The woman had been pestering Eleanora to donate a five-acre site on prime land near the harbor for a new library, which Jemima wished to name after her deceased father. "After all," Jemima had stated as she'd crossed her arms defensively, "the land should rightly have been mine, and I'd say you owe me far more, seeing as how you as good as stole it from my father."

Stole it?

Eleanora sat up straighter. She sniffed, deciding that poor Jemima was just jealous. The Winthrops had once been a wealthy family in these parts, owning plenty of land around River Bend until Jemima's daddy's granary had gone belly up. Yes, Marvin had snapped up the company as well as most of the Winthrops' assets for a song, but that hardly seemed reason for Jemima to act as if Eleanora was the cause of all her family's woes.

. . . you owe me. . .

"Ha," Eleanora said out loud. She didn't owe the Winthrops a thing.

She picked up her spectacles and unfolded them, propping them upon her nose as she went through the letters one by one.

"Miss Nora?"

She glanced up to see Zelma standing in the doorway. "What is it?"

"It's your daughter-in-law, Miss Jean. She said she

heard about your close call this morning, and she's come to see you. She's waiting in the kitchen."

"Jean's here?" Eleanora's spine stiffened. The blood drained from her face. "I told you she wasn't welcome in my house," she got out, her voice trembling, "not after what she did to my son."

"But, Miss Nora, don't you think you've . . . "

"No!" Eleanora cut off Zelma with a sweep of her hand. "Send her away!"

"Yes, ma'am," the housekeeper murmured.

Of all the nerve, Eleanora fumed, her hands shaking, wondering what in heaven's name would bring Jean over to see her. Hadn't she done enough harm already? Hadn't she brought enough pain?

It had been Jean at the wheel when she and Jim had swerved off the Great River Road into the guardrail along the Mississippi River. Jean had driven them home from Jerseyville after Jim's visit with the ophthalmologist. The rain had made the road slick, and Jim had apparently asked Jean to drive because the drops in his eyes had made it hard for him to see. Jean had missed turning onto the back road to River Bend and had ended up in Elsah before getting onto the freeway. She claimed a pickup had veered across the lanes and she'd jerked at the wheel to avoid a crash. Their SUV had jumped the median, slammed into the guardrail, and flipped on the opposite side of the highway. The police had investigated but had never been able to track down the truck or drum up a single witness. Jean had emerged from the wreck with nary a scratch, but Jim had been crushed like a rag doll. He'd been dead on arrival at the hospital.

Eleanora's eyes blurred, and she blinked against the tears.

As far as she was concerned, Jean had killed Jim, and Eleanora had no intention of ever forgiving her. Even if a coroner's inquest had let Jean off the hook, Eleanora knew the truth. If not for Jean, her son would be alive and well.

With a sniff, Eleanora pulled off her specs and set them aside, wiping the damp from her lashes with the back of her hand. Children weren't supposed to die before their mothers. That wasn't how the good Lord meant for it to happen.

She pushed away from the desk. Her head hurt as well as her heart, and she wanted nothing more than to lie down for a spell. The day had already been a rough one by anyone's standards.

Glancing at Lady curled up on the nearby chair cushion, she figured a catnap might just be the thing for her, too. She'd only just settled herself down on the Queen Anne sofa, a chintz-covered pillow propped under her head, when Zelma appeared.

"Miss Nora?"

She sniffed. "What is it this time?"

Zelma rubbed her hands on her apron, her thin shoulders stooping. "It's Miss Winthrop, ma'am. Said she got wind of what happened to you earlier, and she wanted to discuss the land . . . "

" . . . in case someone should try to run me over again?" Eleanora finished for her, resting her forearm on her brow, feeling the throbbing at her temples grow tenfold.

"Should I tell her that you're indisposed?"

"Say whatever you want, Zelma, I don't care," Eleanora snapped. "Just get rid of her, you hear me?"

"Yes, ma'am." Zelma ducked out of the room as noise-lessly as she'd come.

So Jemima Winthrop had dropped by as well? Probably wanted to check and see if her pulse was still beating. Eleanora scowled. That woman would love nothing better than to find her with one foot in the grave. As if that might make Eleanora change her mind about giving in to Jemima's whims when River Bend already had a perfectly good library as it was. She was just testing her, Eleanora knew, just pulling at her to see if the guilt she piled on as thick as clam chowder would break Eleanora down.

She closed her eyes and sighed, somehow managing to nod off, though it seemed she'd slept but a few minutes when she felt a hand on her shoulder, shaking.

"Miss Nora?"

She forced open her eyelids to see Zelma's owlish face hovering. Breath that smelled of minty Polident rustled her hair. "What now?" she asked groggily. "Well, go on, I don't have all day."

"I'm sorry, ma'am, I told him you were napping."

"Told who?" Eleanora raised her head from the pillow and sat up.

"It's Mr. Duncan."

Stanley was in town? Eleanora ground her teeth. Lord above, what could Marvin's brother want now? As if she needed to ask. She knew the answer as surely as she knew her own name.

Money.

Stan had managed to squander away the inheritance Marvin had left him, blowing it on foolish investments and gambling on the *Alton Belle*. Eleanora had written him a check or two just to keep him out of her hair, but she was tired of bailing him out.

"He wouldn't leave, ma'am, not even when I mentioned your being out like a light. I gave him a cup of coffee in the kitchen. He insists on speaking to you, Miss Nora."

"I'm sure he does," she said and gingerly swung her legs over the edge of the couch. She brushed at the wrinkled linen of her slacks, not even glancing up at Zelma as she announced, "Tell him the bank is closed."

"The bank is closed?" Zelma repeated.

"If he wants a penny more, he'll have to wait till I'm gone."

Zelma looked confused but uttered, "Yes, ma'am." Then she disappeared from the library once more.

All the comings and goings apparently disturbed Lady Godiva, for the cat let out an unhappy-sounding mew. Eleanora pushed up and onto her feet. She went over to where the Persian sat poised like a lion atop the Louis XV seat, and she stroked the soft head, watching round eyes blink lovingly then close altogether. She listened as the cat rumbled with pleasure.

Ah, Lady. When Eleanora had lost Marvin, and then Jim so soon thereafter, she'd had a hole in her heart big enough to fit a cannonball. Lady had been her saving grace. Without her precious baby to fuss over and spoil, Eleanora would have come apart at the seams. Lady's presence made her feel somehow at peace. Zelma claimed she went overboard on the feline, but Eleanora disagreed. Lady demanded only her affection, which was a lot less than most people.

"Miss Nora?"

Dear God. What now? Would she never have five minutes to herself?

"What?" Eleanora ceased petting the cat and straightened up with a sigh.

Even Lady turned her pale eyes on Zelma and hissed.

The housekeeper hung back in the doorway. "It's Floyd Baskin, ma'am. He said he heard you'd nearly been run over."

"And he wanted to see if I was on my deathbed, just like the rest," Eleanora remarked rather snippily.

"I gave him a cup of coffee, ma'am."

"Well, take it back and send him off!"

Zelma bobbed her head, the tufts of faded brown hardly hiding her scalp. The light reflected off her glasses so that for a moment she looked eerily like a blank-eyed Orphan Annie. Then, without another word, she did an about-face and disappeared.

Eleanora braced a hand on the arm of the chair, trying to steady herself, wondering who could possibly be next; perhaps an agent from the IRS come to audit her?

First there was Jean, then Jemima and Stanley, and now Floyd Baskin. Was there a national holiday regarding mortal enemies dropping in that Eleanora didn't know about?

She shuffled over to the desk and settled into Marvin's old chair again, leaning her head back against the soft leather.

Floyd Baskin ran a group called Save the River which, upon its inception, had quietly worked to clean up the more-than-muddy Mississippi. In those days, half a dozen years before, Baskin had seemed a dedicated and idealistic fellow, and Marvin had contributed often and generously to the cause. Even in death, Marvin had provided an annual stipend to Save the River. But Eleanora knew that if Marvin had lived, he wouldn't have wanted to give Baskin another dime.

The man had turned radical. He broke into the power plants that operated along the river and set off smoke bombs. He spray-painted threatening graffiti on walls and left dead fish on doormats.

No, Eleanora mused, clasping her hands on the desktop. Marvin would hardly support Baskin's newfound terroristic tactics, and she was going to do everything she could to cut him off. She had her lawyers working on it now, and Baskin knew it. Even his constant begging, desperate letters, and frantic telephone calls wouldn't work, not if Eleanora had anything to say about it.

"Miss Nora?"

"For God's sake!" She shook off her thoughts and glared at Zelma, who shrank perceptibly beneath her stare. "What is it this time? Not another visitor? What is this place, Grand Central Station? Even Calvin Coolidge managed to find a few hours to nap every day, and he was president, for crying out loud!"

"They're all gone, Miss Nora." The tiny eyes behind the lenses blinked. "It's time for Lady Godiva's supper."

Eleanora glanced at her wristwatch. "You're right, it is."

Zelma started across the room toward the cat, but Lady hopped off the chair before Zelma got near enough to grab her. With a swish of tail, she darted under the desk, hiding by Eleanora's feet.

"I'll take care of her," Eleanora offered. "Oh, and Zelma, fix me up a plate of something as well. I haven't had a bite to eat since breakfast. What with nearly being killed and all, I completely forgot about lunch."

"Yes, ma'am."

As soon as the housekeeper was out of sight, Lady Godiva bounded into Eleanora's lap. "C'mon, precious," she cooed, rising to her feet with the cat in her arms. "Soup's on."

Chapter 3

HELEN SET DOWN the saucer heaped with the contents of a can of Liver 'n' Chicken. Her oversized yellow tom took a single sniff before shaking his tail at her and glancing up with pleading eyes, as if to say, *Isn't there something better than this?*

"No," she told him, trying hard to be firm. "You're getting too finicky in your old age, Amber. This was your favorite last week, remember?"

But apparently he'd forgotten.

He mewed at her in a sharp tone not unlike a child back-talking. Then he padded out of the kitchen, tail straight in the air as if to let her know he wasn't happy in the least with her decision.

Good grief, she thought, shaking her head as she watched him go. No wonder there were plenty of folks who preferred dogs to felines. A pup ate whatever he was given and seemed glad for it, slobbering happily when he was done. Cats balked when you accidently fed them the same kind of canned food twice in a row. It was the fault of the Egyptians, she decided, wiping off her hands on her sweatpants. She couldn't blame the furry creatures for expecting a lot. She would, too, if she'd once been worshipped as a god by the likes of Cleopatra.

She smiled, figuring Amber was spoiled almost as much as that. And to think she'd very nearly missed out on having a cat altogether.

In all the years she and Joe had been married—all the while their kids had been growing up—he'd been dead set against having an animal of any sort. "They're dirty," he'd said, "they shed like mad, and they stink."

Helen shook her head even now at the memory.

When their children had moved away and started raising families of their own, Joe had broken down and agreed—though not without grumbling—to let her adopt a stray that their granddaughter, Nancy, had found one summer years ago. She'd named the cat Amber because of the color of his eyes. No dummy he, Amber had instantly attached himself to Joe, crawling into his lap whenever it was empty, rubbing against his calves, sleeping near his feet atop the bedspread. Pretty soon it was Joe who'd woken up to feed Amber in the mornings, who'd cleaned up the bunny guts Amber had left on the porch. So when Joe had died three years ago, Helen knew she wasn't the only one who'd mourned his absence. Amber hadn't been himself for months after.

Helen sighed and pushed up her sleeves. She turned

on the tap at the sink, the pipes squealing as the water gushed out. She stuck her hands beneath, soaping them up to erase the smell of Liver 'n' Chicken. She glanced down at the rejected saucer of cat food and clicked tongue against teeth, thinking some humans probably didn't eat so well as her spoiled tomcat. Though Helen was hardly undernourished herself, she realized she hadn't had a bite since breakfast, save for the cheese ball she'd snatched at Jean's earlier in the day, so just about anything sounded good to her at the moment.

She averted her eyes from Amber's untouched dinner and opened the refrigerator door. There wasn't much to look at inside beyond half a cantaloupe, a doggy bag from the Denny's in Alton, and a nearly expired carton of milk.

When *was* the last time she'd gotten to the grocery store?

She'd had so many bridge games lately, not to mention the planning sessions of the Ladies Civic Improvement League and a smattering of other causes entailing lunches and dinners out, that she'd put off making a supermarket run.

She retrieved several slices of American cheese that, upon close inspection, hadn't yet hardened around the edges. She scrounged up the remnants of a tub of butter and two slices of bread—a little hard, but no mold— deciding a grilled cheese would have to do.

The phone rang, and she dropped her stash on the countertop, hurrying to hush the darned thing before it whistled again like a demented bird.

"Hello?"

Jean Duncan's voice filled her ear. "Helen? Have you eaten yet?"

She recalled the smell of Jean's kitchen, the taste of the olive-stuffed cheese puff, and her stomach growled. "No, not yet," she told her, praying some kind of invitation was forthcoming.

"How'd you like to meet me at the diner for one of Erma's meat loaf sandwiches? After working in the kitchen half the day, I'm tired of the sight of anything even remotely gourmet."

Well, Helen mused, meat loaf at the diner wasn't exactly what she'd hoped for, but it would do in a pinch. "Five minutes, okay?"

Jean laughed. "Are you gonna fly there or walk?"

Helen grinned, switching the receiver to her other ear. "See you shortly," she said and hung up at Jean's "All right."

Before she left, she ran a brush through her wiry gray hair, taming it as best she could. She did a quick tooth-brushing, rinsing out her mouth and patting it dry. She put on a dab of pink lipstick then grabbed up her purse and left.

Between the craggy bluffs on the town's either side, she could see the vague purple ribbons of sunset fading from the sky as twilight moved in, giving the stars a dark background to wink against.

The streetlights had come on, lending an orange glow to the sidewalk as she strode ahead past picket fences and neatly kept lawns. Tulip bulbs planted before the first freeze last November now sprouted upward, their colorful buds about ready to pop.

A dog barked from a screened-in porch, the high-pitched yips soon joined by mournful baying from another backyard.

Helen picked up her steps, her Keds crunching over the stray gravel kicked onto the sidewalk by cars rolling up and down Jersey en route to Main Street.

She inhaled deeply as she walked, breathing in fresh air tinged by the muddy odor of the river dead ahead. Lights shone through the windows of the houses she passed, and she spied more than a few heads bent over kitchen tables between parted curtains. At lunchtime, the streets seemed similarly empty when the carillon in the chapel's steeple played its programmed tunes over loudspeakers and everyone within earshot scattered, heading home or to the diner for a sandwich.

Despite the changes that had come over River Bend in recent years, much had remained as it was almost fifty years ago when she and Joe had settled here. It was one of the main reasons Helen had never moved away. Maybe it was her age, but she'd come to like knowing what each day brought. She liked the familiarity of faces, the languid pace. All the changes she wanted to see were those wrought by the seasons. She loved the starkness of winter when ice clung to eaves and branches and snow blanketed rooftops and roads. The summers seemed at times like a photograph overexposed, the sun so bright the air looked yellow. Dust from the roads covered shrubs and boats filled the river, drawing skiers across the brown waters. In the fall, the trees turned every shade of red and gold imaginable, and cars came from across the river—St. Louis and beyond—just to witness the unbearable beauty of the bluffs.

Helen decided she liked spring best of all except for the years when the rains fell too fast and the river rose too quickly, flooding the town and making a canoe the favored mode of transportation, River Bend seemed at its best dressed in green. It took away her breath to see the foliage on the bluffs so verdant against the chalky façades. Cicadas hummed their nightly tune from unseen places. Owls hooted plaintively, and whippoorwills joined the chorus. There was just a hint of a chill in the night air.

Why, she wondered, would anyone want to live anywhere else?

Downtown, the parallel rows of shops that ran barely two blocks were fronted with barrels bursting with pansies and petunias, signs of the Ladies Civic Improvement League in action.

There was the drugstore and corner grocery, the one-pump gas station, the stationery store, and the sheriff's office next door to Agnes March's antiques shop. All were dark save for the diner. Its plate glass window spilled light onto the sidewalk.

The door jingled as she entered, leaving the stillness of the night for the swell of voices.

"Helen! Over here!"

She looked across the crowded room to see Jean waving from a booth in the far corner.

Others bid her hello as well, and she paused to exchange quick greetings with each. Erma swept past in her checkerboard pink uniform, five hot plates balanced on her arms. Still, she managed a grin and a friendly, "Hey, there, Helen, be right with ya."

Erma had been at the diner for as long as Helen could remember and never seemed to have a bit of trouble doing two things at once.

Sheriff Frank Biddle swiveled about on a stool at the counter and ceased filling his mouth with French fries long enough to nod at Helen. His wife, Sarah, was out of town for a day or two, visiting her mother in Springfield. Helen didn't doubt that Erma would feed the town's sole lawman morning, noon, and dusk while his better half was gone.

"You're right on time," Jean remarked as Helen sat down.

"And I'm starving," Helen confessed.

Her friend sipped coffee, a plastic-coated menu at her left elbow. Helen snagged it before slipping glasses from her purse. Once she had her specs perched on her nose, she opened the menu to study the taped-on note about the day's specials.

"You get a chance to see Eleanora?" she asked and peered over the menu as a frown erased the smile from Jean's mouth.

"She wouldn't let me past the kitchen," Jean admitted and set her coffee down, keeping her hands around the mug as if to warm them. "Nothing's changed as far as she's concerned, the old bat."

"Now Jean," Helen softly scolded.

"Well, it's true."

"You didn't give her the food you'd made?"

Jean fiddled with the scarf tied round her ponytail. "I put everything in Mother-in-law Dearest's fridge. Though, let me tell you, I was tempted to just turn around and bring it home."

"You did the right thing," Helen said and reached out to pat her friend's hand. But Jean wouldn't meet her eyes.

The noise of a throat being cleared drew Helen's attention up, and she removed her specs to find herself staring into the weathered face of Frank Biddle.

"Sheriff," she said, noting the ketchup at the corner of his mouth and the spot on his brown tie as well.

"Hello, Frank," Jean greeted him.

"Mrs. Duncan," he said as the ceiling lamps glanced off the thinning spot atop his hatless head.

"Uh, Mrs. Evans," he said, meeting Helen's gaze directly. He set a palm on the table and leaned over. "I heard you were witness to an accident this morning."

"What accident?" Helen set the menu down.

"Mrs. Duncan," he told her, looking at Jean for an instant. His cheeks flushed. "No, I mean, old Mrs. Duncan."

Jean stared into her coffee.

Helen wished he hadn't brought the subject up. "It wasn't an accident exactly, Sheriff," she said, hoping to clear things up quickly as Jean was looking decidedly uncomfortable. "Eleanora stepped off the curb and a car narrowly missed her, but no one was hurt." Helen tapped her fingers on the table. "She was rather frightened though."

Biddle straightened up and scratched at his jaw. His wide brow wrinkled as though he'd contemplated her answer and found it lacking. "You see the driver, ma'am?" he asked. "Did you get the plate numbers? How about the make and model of the car?"

Helen laughed. "Sheriff, it happened so fast, I didn't have a chance to do much but pull Eleanora out of harm's way."

"Did you notice the color, ma'am?"

She exhaled slowly. "It was filthy, that's all I do remember. What with the rains we've had, everything's kind of muddy."

"And?" he prodded.

"Well, it might have been blue," she said.

He nodded.

"Or it could have been brown."

He raised his eyebrows.

Helen felt as if she'd failed a test. His face seemed so filled with disappointment. She looked across the table at Jean, who'd paled considerably in the past minute or two. "Look, Sheriff, I don't know any more except that maybe it was an older model sedan."

He crossed his arms above his belly, which hung low over his gun belt and strained the buttons on his tan uniform shirt. "That doesn't narrow it down much, Mrs. Evans, since it probably describes most of the cars around town."

"Sorry."

He ducked his chin, muttering, "Ma'am," which Helen

knew was meant to encompass them both. Then he sauntered back to his stool, his hat marking his space on the
counter. He settled back down and resumed his attack on
the French fries.

Helen turned to Jean and reached across the table.
"Don't let it get to you, all right? We're here for supper,
aren't we?"

Jean sighed. "I know I shouldn't let anything about Eleanora bother me anymore, but still it's . . . "

The door flew open, pushed so wide it banged the wall.
The bells above it jangled violently.

"Sheriff!" a voice cried out. "Sheriff Biddle!"

Helen glanced across the room to where Zelma Burdine stood with her hands at her breasts, panting, as if
she'd run to the diner without stopping.

"Sheriff!" she shouted again, her owlish eyes looking
this way and that, as if unable to make out Frank Biddle
at the counter.

He hopped down abruptly, knocking over his glass and
sending Erma darting in his direction with a towel. He
shrugged away her ministrations and, thumbs hooked in
his belt, strode over to the trembling Zelma.

"What seems to be the trouble, ma'am?" he asked,
and Helen noticed the silence that hung in the air, as she
waited along with the rest of the diner to hear Zelma's
response.

The woman hugged her arms around her middle and
choked out between tears, "Something's happened . . . oh,
my . . . something awful."

"What's that, ma'am?" the sheriff asked.

"Miss Nora," she cried, wringing her hands, "She isn't moving. Please, you've got to help."

Helen turned to Jean, but her friend didn't meet her gaze. She acted as if she hadn't even heard Zelma's pleas. Instead, she raised her cup of coffee to her mouth and took a long, slow sip.

Chapter 4

THROUGH THE PLATE glass window of the diner, Helen watched Biddle lead Zelma toward his squad car and help her into the front seat before he slipped in on the driver's side. In another moment, the black-and-white was gone, tires spitting gravel in their wake.

Though the rest of the diner seemed to settle down again, utensils clattering as everyone's attention returned to their food, Helen found she'd lost her appetite.

She pushed her glasses into her purse then tucked the handbag into the crook of her elbow. The vinyl of the bench squeaked as she slid out of the booth.

Jean set down her mug with a clatter, and Helen paused as her friend spoke up. "We haven't even ordered, and you're leaving already? Please, don't tell me you're going over to Eleanora's to find out what she's done now."

"Aren't you even the least bit curious?"

"Absolutely not," her friend said, her tone laced with

bitterness. "No, I'm finished with worrying about Eleanora. As far as I'm concerned, she's out of my life for good."

"I'm sorry to hear that," Helen admitted, "and I can't say I blame you. You did try to extend the olive branch, didn't you? She was the one who wouldn't leave the past alone."

Jean didn't respond. She toyed with her cup of coffee, though she made no move to drink it.

"We'll talk soon," Helen said and left the booth, making her way through the aisles between the tables and exiting the diner in a jingle of bells.

The night air felt good against her face, the faint breeze from the river tugging gently at her hair, its crispness quickening her pace.

The Duncan house was but a couple blocks away, though it seemed a world apart in some respects. Tidy one-story houses with clapboard façades and tiny yards followed one after another with hardly a picnic table's width between. Until the street curved away, bending past the harbor where a dozen or so small boats were docked, and the homes seemed overgrown suddenly and an acre apart at least.

There were no picket fences here, no yapping dogs or front lawns filled with bicycles and children's toys. Not a single dented Chevy or compact car sat parked upon the gravel-strewn road.

Though River Bend was home to young and old, rich and poor, Helen knew that most of its citizens had surpassed middle age years ago. Few were without some sort of nest egg to live on. But the residents of Harbor Drive had more than IRAs and monthly pensions to draw from. Like Eleanora Duncan, those who lived on this street of French colonials and Victorians had deep pockets that only time and trust funds could so amply fill.

Helen spotted Biddle's car up ahead, beneath the towering oak she'd seen Eleanora leaning against just that morning.

She hurried up the sidewalk to the path that led directly to the whitewashed Victorian with its encircling porch, noting that the windows facing front were all aglow.

Her breaths grew noisy as she climbed the steps and crossed to the door. The planked boards beneath her feet creaked and groaned with every stride.

She paused to inhale deeply once and then twice, trying hard to slow her racing heart.

What if Eleanora was hurt, she thought as she picked up the brass knocker and thumped it several times. What if she'd fallen and couldn't get up? Heaven knew, with all those stairs leading up three floors, it very well could have happened. This house was too big for Eleanora to live in alone. Helen had discussed the very subject with her a time or two, but Eleanora didn't want to move. "It's my home," she'd insisted. "Where else would I go?" At which point, Helen hadn't had the heart to say another word.

The door came open suddenly, and Helen stood nose to nose with Frank Biddle.

His face fell at the sight of her. "Oh, it's you," he said, but, when she frowned at him, he added, "I thought it might be Doc Melville. I phoned him as soon as I saw."

"Saw what?" Helen tried to peer over his shoulder, but all she could make out was the empty foyer. Although she did hear a noise. Was that someone crying?

She pushed past him. "For goodness' sake, Sheriff, where's Eleanora? Is that her sobbing? What in God's name is going on?"

She followed the sounds, ignoring Biddle's attempts to thwart her progress.

Crossing the dining room and rounding the Chippendale table and chairs, she pushed through a swinging door that opened into the kitchen.

"Ma'am, please stay back." Biddle tried to get her to stop for the umpteenth time, but Helen didn't listen. If Eleanora needed help—and obviously she did, or the sheriff wouldn't have telephoned Doc Melville—then she was going to do what she could until he got here, even if it meant little more than holding a hand or plumping a pillow.

"No, no, no! Jesus, Joseph, and Mary, no . . . "

Across the room was Zelma, down on her knees and shivering, crying into the hem of her apron. Helen took a step forward.

Biddle's hand gripped her arm. "Ma'am, please. . . . "

Helen brushed off his fingers and kept walking, around a heavy butcher's block and past the length of white Formica countertop still cluttered with what appeared to be preparations for dinner.

Zelma rocked on her heels. Her huge round glasses were steamy with tears.

Helen forced her own gaze downward.

"Eleanora?" she tried to say, but the name caught in her throat.

The familiar white hair that was always so perfectly coiffed looked tousled. Her head was propped up by a rolled kitchen towel, eyes wide and fixed ceiling-ward. Her features were contorted like a Halloween mask, the drooping skin carved with lines that crossed her cheeks and brow.

"Good God," Helen breathed, taking a step back and turning to Biddle. "Is she dead?" she asked, though she realized what he'd say before he said it.

The sheriff had removed his hat and tucked it under his arm. Grimly, he nodded. "I'm afraid so, ma'am."

She felt her stomach knot. "What," she sputtered, "what happened? Was it a heart attack or stroke?"

"That's why I called Doc," was all he'd tell her.

Footsteps sounded beyond the swinging door, and Amos Melville appeared, leather satchel in hand. White hair fell over his wrinkled brow, nearly reaching the arch of his bushy brows. His spectacles perched low on his nose, and his eyes peered above them, alert and anxious.

The sheriff jumped right in, explaining, "I figured she might just be unconscious, but I checked her out myself, Doc. I put an ear to her chest to see if she was still breathing. I even stuck a spoon under her nose, but it didn't cloud up a bit. Even CPR couldn't have saved her since it was clear she was already gone."

"Where is she?" Amos asked.

Sheriff Biddle gestured over to where Eleanora lay on the floor. Helen stepped aside, but Zelma wasn't as willing to move away. She shook her head when Doc tried to guide her to her feet.

Biddle started walking over to help, but Helen lifted a hand, stopping him with a stern gaze. She set aside her purse and turned to Zelma, talking softly to the woman, telling her that Doc was there to help Eleanora, not to hurt her. Finally, with a great sigh, Zelma came up off the floor, and Helen put an arm around her thin shoulders, leading her aside so Doc had room enough to work.

He plunked down his bag and reached for Eleanora, gently probing at her neck and then her wrists for a pulse. He pulled a stethoscope from the satchel, hooked it in his ears, and pressed it to several spots on her chest and throat. With a click of tongue on teeth, he put away the device. Then he checked Eleanora's eyes with his penlight, asking without looking up, "How long did you say she's been like this?"

Biddle shifted on his feet. "Ten minutes at least."

"And before you arrived?" Doc wanted to know as he lifted each of Eleanora's hands to study her fingernails, then prodded her abdomen and thereabouts.

Zelma sniffled loudly before she spoke up in a quavering tone, "Miss Nora took a snack back with her to the library while I fixed her supper. It was about an hour ago, I'd guess. She came to get me a few minutes after, moaning about her head and her stomach. I figured she'd eaten something that'd disagreed with her. Miss Nora had a sensitive digestive tract. I tried to watch her diet for her."

Zelma hiccupped, and Helen tightened her hold on the woman. The housekeeper calmed down enough to further explain, "I left her there"—she pointed to the oak table and surrounding chairs, one of which had tipped onto its side—"and I went after the Pepto. I couldn't have been gone for more than a minute. But when I got back, she was doubled over, hollering for help. She fell to the floor and started twitching." Zelma shuddered and twisted the hem of her apron, as if remembering was too unbearable. "Oh, dear, but it was horrible to watch. I tried to hold her still to make her stop."

Doc nodded, and gently lifted Eleanora's head to take the towel from beneath. He unfurled the checkered terry cloth and covered the dead woman's face.

Though Doc Melville was near her own age, Helen thought he looked a dozen years more than that now. Like her, he'd known the Duncans for years, and being too late to do anything for poor Eleanora couldn't have sat easy with him.

He quietly closed up his bag and stood. He put his satchel on the counter and looked at Biddle. "If you don't mind, Sheriff, I'd like to give Ed Drake a call, have him take the body into Jerseyville."

Dr. Drake, Helen knew, was the medical examiner for Jersey County. She felt her heart race, understanding what it meant for him to be summoned.

"You think she was murdered?" Biddle asked the very

thing Helen had been wondering herself. He turned his hat around in his hands and went on, "I'm only bringing it up because of her nearly getting run down this morning. Maybe someone was trying to get even with her."

"Sheriff, please," Helen scolded, looking at him sideways. Somehow it didn't sit right for him to be speculating out loud about murder when Eleanora was a few feet away on the floor and Zelma near enough to hear every word.

"You said it yourself, ma'am," the sheriff said, not letting go. "The car came out of nowhere. And people like Mrs. Duncan, well, sometimes all that money and power make for plenty of enemies."

Helen glared at him, wishing he'd hush up, as Zelma had started to shake all over again.

Doc went to the sink and washed his hands, talking over the flow of the water. "I'm not about to make any judgments one way or the other, not yet anyhow. It could very well have been something Eleanora ate. She might've had some allergy none of us were aware of. Old age does funny things to us all, which is why I don't like to second-guess in this type of situation."

He turned off the tap and shook his hands as he glanced around him, though the only towel in evidence was the one he'd used to cover Eleanora's face. He ended up wiping his palms on his trousers, leaving wet streaks on the tan. Then he pushed the hair back from his brow and quietly said, "No, I'd hate to speculate, no matter what my suspicions. So I won't. Not till after Drake's done an examination."

"There'll be an autopsy?" Zelma spoke up, as if only

then realizing what all the talk meant. She looked first at Helen, then at Doc and Biddle. "Oh, dear, they're not gonna cut into Miss Nora like a side of roast beef?"

The sheriff cleared his throat and stared down at his shoes.

Amos seemed similarly at a loss for words.

Helen gently turned Zelma so that she faced her. "Dr. Drake will take very good care of her, I'm sure. He just needs to determine what caused"—she glanced toward the body, dishtowel draped like a shroud over the face—"what caused this to happen," she finished.

Though Zelma whimpered, she appeared to accept Eleanora's fate.

A quiet mewing noise drew Helen's attention toward the door leading in from the pantry. There on the threshold stood Lady Godiva.

Round copper eyes looked up, and the plump tail twitched. Then the cat tiptoed into the kitchen and headed straight toward Eleanora. She paused and sniffed at the dishtowel, circling the body once before lifting her head and howling mournfully.

Zelma burst into tears.

The sheriff and Amos both stared at Helen.

"C'mon, dear, let's go sit down in another room," she told Zelma, glad for the chance to leave the kitchen and the horrid sight of Lady crying over Eleanora.

As Helen urged Zelma through the rear pantry, she saw Doc pick up the phone. "This way," she said as they followed the hallway and ducked into the first open door.

"I, can't believe it," Zelma sobbed as Helen sat her down on a settee in a yellow-walled living room. "I can't believe she's gone."

Helen patted her hand, whispering words meant to soothe, all the while thinking of what Biddle had said a moment ago: that Eleanora's near accident was, perhaps, no accident. That someone might have wanted Eleanora Duncan out of the picture for good.

Chapter 5

BIDDLE POKED HIS head into the room not ten minutes after.

"Boys from the medical examiner's are here," he said, standing stiffly near the doorway. He had his shoulders squared, and his belly overlapped his gun belt.

Helen nodded at him from the velvet-covered settee, all the while patting Zelma's knee.

"It shouldn't take long to get things, uh, bagged up," Biddle added, though Helen wished he'd put it more delicately.

The housekeeper tensed at his words. Her eyes, red and swollen behind her round lenses, stared down at the twisted tissue she gripped with trembling fingers.

"Uh, Miss Burdine." The sheriff took a few steps in, paused, and hiked up his pants. "The forensics team . . . they need to know what Mrs. Duncan was eating before she got sick. You said she had a snack in the library?"

Zelma dabbed at her nose. "Yes, that's right," she said,

her voice soft and ragged. "She fed the cat before getting something from the fridge for herself." The housekeeper stared down at her feet. "She got a box of wafers from the cabinet. Said she'd missed lunch because of what happened this morning."

"Mind if we gather up a few things, ma'am?" Biddle asked.

Zelma shook her head, her eyes downcast. "Take whatever you need." She shredded the tissue into half a dozen pieces. "It doesn't matter anymore. Nothing matters."

The sheriff scratched his jaw, looking as uncomfortable as Helen had ever seen him. He opened his mouth as if to say something more but seemed to reconsider and ducked out of the room instead.

Helen glimpsed him passing the room a moment later with another man in tow.

"Don't worry, Zelma, everything will be fine, you'll see," she said, hardly believing a word of it herself. "The sheriff and Doc Melville will take care of everything. They'll find out what happened to Eleanora soon enough. And then you can start getting your life back to normal."

Zelma raised her chin, the loose skin of her neck quivering as she met Helen's eyes head-on with her Coke-bottle stare. "Back to normal?" she repeated, her voice a mere squeak. "Normal, you say?" Tears swam down cheeks already blotched pink by her crying. "You don't seem to understand. She was all I had, Mrs. Evans. I don't have kin of my own. I never married," she added, whispering, "Miss Nora always told me she was all the family I'd need."

"I'm sorry, Zelma. Truly I am," Helen apologized, feeling like a heel, not having realized until then how much Eleanora Duncan had meant to the woman. Helen had known Eleanora as well as anyone, in the way that those in a small town know who everyone is and what they're up to. None of the Duncans, save for Jim, had ever been easy to get close to. Eleanora and Marvin had seemed to prefer keeping to themselves. When Eleanora had lost her husband and, soon after, her son, she'd seemed to draw even more tightly into her cocoon, emerging only when she'd felt obligated to attend a committee meeting. After what had happened this morning—the near miss that Sheriff Biddle seemed to think was suspicious—and after Zelma's confession, Helen suddenly realized how little she truly knew of Eleanora beyond the local gossip and their brief encounters at luncheons and whatnot.

"Tell me something, Zelma," she said and lowered her voice to the same soothing tone she'd used on grandchildren with skinned knees, "did Eleanora have any other accidents before the one this morning? Any other close calls?"

"Close calls?" Zelma reared her head, her brow squishing up like an accordion. "I'm not sure I know what you mean."

Helen thought of telling Zelma what Eleanora had said to her earlier. *I think somebody's trying to kill me* had been her exact words. But she reconsidered, asking only, "Had she been threatened?"

"Threatened?" Zelma's blotchy face drained of all color.

"Why, you don't really believe someone meant to harm Miss Nora?"

Helen sighed, setting her hands in her lap. "I honestly don't know," she said. But Eleanora had obviously felt that the driver of the car had meant to run her down. Her passing this evening could most certainly have been caused by old age itself. But Amos Melville's hesitation at pronouncing a cause of death made Helen reluctant to dismiss Biddle's remarks altogether. Doc knew his business as well as any general practitioner from here to Joplin. For him to call for an autopsy of an eighty-year-old widow who'd died in her own kitchen must mean that he, too, felt something was amiss or at least worth looking into.

"It shouldn't have happened," Zelma murmured, her sobs cutting off her words now and again like hiccups. "She shouldn't have died on me."

Helen absently patted Zelma's hand, all the while looking around her at the richly appointed room with its intricate crown molding and limestone fireplace. She gazed at oil paintings in gilded frames hung upon the dramatic canary-colored walls, at shelves filled with leather-bound books, and rich cherry tables topped with Tiffany lamps and assorted crystal pieces. Everything she saw looked of museum quality.

And suddenly she found herself wondering who would inherit the substantial fortune of an old woman whose husband and son had predeceased her.

She heard footsteps and glanced toward the open door to catch another fellow in dark clothes with a black bag going in the same direction the sheriff and a crime scene investigator had gone earlier.

Helen swallowed. Her throat felt tight. It seemed unbelievable to even consider that there might have been foul play involved in Eleanora's demise.

"Miss Nora hired me when I was just sixteen. She hadn't even gotten married yet. Did you know that, ma'am?" Zelma asked, breaking through Helen's thoughts.

She turned to Zelma and smiled gently. "I'm afraid I didn't, no."

The housekeeper pushed up from the settee. She collected the bits of torn tissue from her lap and stuck them in her apron pocket. She shuffled over to the mantel, where a host of silver-framed photographs perched, and picked out the largest from the bunch. Helen glimpsed a black-and-white shot of a baby with a spit curl. Zelma let out a cry and hugged it to her bosom.

"Mr. Jim . . . he was such a good boy," she said. "Miss Nora doted on him. It near to killed her when he died. She never forgave Miss Jean. She blamed her till the end."

Helen sighed. "That I do know, yes."

"Miss Jean came by today and brought all that food, but Miss Nora wouldn't even give her the time of day."

So Jean had mentioned at the diner, Helen recalled, knowing how much courage it had taken for Jean to come to Eleanora like that, and what a slap in the face it must have been when Eleanora had turned her away. Forgiveness didn't always come easily.

Only now it was too late for them to make up, wasn't it?

With a clatter, Zelma set the picture of Jim back amidst the others then walked slowly about the room. She touched a bronzed statuette, wiped a bit of dust off the corner of a table with the hem of her apron, and brushed at the cushion of a Queen Anne wing chair as though out of habit. Then she broke down again.

Helen got up and went to her, turning her around and settling her down into the chair.

"Oh, dear," Zelma murmured between sobs. "What'll become of her?"

Helen patted her shoulder. "Please, try not to worry about Eleanora. Amos will keep tabs on her."

"No." Zelma toyed with her tearstained apron. "No, I mean what'll happen to Lady Godiva?"

"Oh, the cat," Helen said, having nearly forgotten about her. The way the poor Persian had wailed when she'd found Eleanora there on the kitchen floor. . . . Helen shuddered at the picture. She remembered how withdrawn Amber had been after Joe's death, and she figured it would be much the same with Lady Godiva. No one could convince her that animals didn't sense distress in the people around them, didn't actually feel emotion themselves.

"She loved that cat as if she were a child," Zelma said, weeping. "Pampered her like nothing I've ever seen."

"Nothing will happen to Lady Godiva," Helen assured her, trying hard not to smile at the turn the conversation had taken. "After all, she's got you to look after her, hasn't she?"

Zelma pulled the tattered tissue from her apron pocket and blew her nose.

Helen took her by the hand and drew her up from the chair. "Come now, dear," she said and directed the woman toward a scroll-armed sofa quite large enough for Zelma to lie down on. "Why don't you just relax for a while, take off your shoes—that's right—and put up your feet." She wedged a tapestry pillow beneath Zelma's head, and the housekeeper let out a weary sigh. "Here, let me have those," Helen said and reached for Zelma's heavy glasses, gently removing them, though the housekeeper made little noises of protest. "It'll do you good to close your eyes for a moment," Helen assured her, suggesting after, "how about if I get you a cold compress? Or make some tea? That'll calm you down, I promise."

"All right," Zelma murmured, already sounding sleepy, "if you're sure it's not too much trouble."

"Nonsense." Helen patted her shoulder.

She started to turn, but surprisingly strong fingers caught at her hand.

"You said they might've been out to get her. Well, maybe you're right."

Helen paused, facing Zelma.

The hand released hers.

"She was always telling me, 'Zelma, when you're rich as Midas, everyone wants a piece of you,'" the housekeeper murmured and fiddled with the hem of her apron. She turned her stockinged feet toes in. "Even today, they wouldn't leave her alone," Zelma whispered. "That awful Mr. Baskin came by, and Miss Winthrop and Stanley."

"Hush now," Helen told her. "Shut your eyes and try to

think of something pleasant. I'll be back in a jiffy." Sneakers squishing on the Aubusson rug, she left the yellow room and closed the door.

The sheriff and the men from forensics were just coming down the hallway from the library when she emerged.

"Well, did you find anything?" she asked, pausing so she blocked their path. "Anything that looked unusual?"

"Just what the housekeeper said we would," Biddle answered and nodded at the pair who grasped labeled evidence bags in latex-gloved hands. Helen could see that one bag held what appeared to be a tin of English biscuits and another held what seemed to be a small plastic container.

"What are those?" she asked.

Biddle hiked up his pants, looking impatiently over her shoulder. "You know I don't like playing guessing games," he said. "So if you don't mind, ma'am, I'll wait till forensics gives me the answers."

"But—" she started, only to have him trample over her attempt to speak.

"Would you excuse us, Mrs. Evans? We've got official business to take care of," he said in a self-important tone, and Helen nodded, stepping aside to let them pass.

She stood there a moment after, watching their retreating backs until they turned left at the end of the hallway. Her stomach knotted, and she suddenly felt a little queasy.

Was it possible that something Eleanora had eaten had killed her? Well, Helen had certainly heard of people dying from salmonella or that E. coli strain every now and again, but it seemed so rare.

So if it wasn't some kind of bacteria that did her in, and if they could find no other natural cause of death, then it must mean . . .

Stop it, she told herself. She was letting her imagination run away again.

Eighty-year-old people died every day without a push, she mused as she headed for the kitchen, trying not to dwell on the fact that most weren't nearly as rich or as powerful as Eleanora was.

Chapter 6

"LADIES! LADIES, CAN I have your attention, *please*."

Voices continued buzzing across town hall despite the desperate plea for quiet. To Helen's ears, the sum of them sounded like an angry swarm of bees.

"Ladies, could I have your . . . aw, hell, girls, would you all just shut up!"

Helen watched mouths pause midsentence as heads turned forward to the podium, where Verna Mabry stood in a pink cotton sheath and matching straw hat. Chairs squeaked as the members of the Ladies Civic Improvement League settled in to listen to their president, though Helen doubted anything Verna had to say would garner nearly as much interest as the news of Eleanora Duncan's demise. Her death the previous night seemed to have already made the rounds on the local grapevine, which was, she thought, much like Superman. *Faster than a speeding bullet.*

"She was past eighty after all"—someone behind her was murmuring—"and she did have a lot of hate in her heart at the end. If you ask me, that's what killed her."

The whispers were quickly stilled by someone's hissed "Hush!"

Perhaps it was a good thing Jean Duncan hadn't shown up, Helen decided as she looked around her, seeing no sign of her friend. She'd tried to call her last evening, but all she'd gotten was Jean's voice mail. It had been the same again this morning.

Ah, well, she figured it would probably just upset Jean to hear the way everyone was talking, which might be the very reason she'd decided to pass on the meeting and try out her gourmet delicacies on the LCIL another time.

"Are we ready now? All right then." Verna Mabry cleared her throat. Her dark gaze peered out from beneath the wide hat brim, which framed a face whose tautness implied intimacy with a surgeon's scalpel; her brow was pulled so tight that she wore a permanent wide-eyed look. Verna shuffled the papers in her hands and announced in her trilling tone, "We are gathered here today to discuss final planning for our annual luncheon. We have the place and time arranged but no one yet to do the food." Verna waved her manicured fingers toward her audience. "Are there any suggestions?"

A blonde in front of Helen popped out of her chair, waggling an arm in the air until Verna inquired, "Yes, dear, what is it?"

"Why don't we have the Catfish Barn cater again?"

Someone behind Helen replied, "Sure, if we want to

get food poisoning," which caused an outbreak of laughter. Even Helen had to chuckle.

"Well, their price is very reasonable," the woman countered before sinking down to her seat, her shoulders slumping.

Verna nodded, the pink hat rocking like a buoy bobbing in rough waters. "Fine idea, Mary Kay, just fine," she chirped. "We'll certainly take it into consideration."

The words elicited more than a few moans. Probably remembrances of the indigestion they'd all suffered last year at the lunch, Helen thought, remembering how the corner market had sold out its stock of Alka-Seltzer within half an hour after.

"How about that new French place in Alton?" a thin brunette hopped up to offer.

Verna Mabry shook her head. "Honey, I've already talked to them, and they're, shall we say, *très* expensive."

"Oh, shoot." The dark-haired woman sat down.

Helen took that moment to rise to her feet. She tugged at the ribbed waist of her purple sweatshirt embroidered with a spray of violets, and Verna's too-wide gaze fixed on her like a guided missile.

"Yes, Helen, what is it?"

"I know just the person to cater." She looked across the faces that turned her way. "How about Jean Duncan?" she said and smiled eagerly. "She's just started her own business, and she's a marvelous cook. I'd hoped she'd show up this morning with some samples, but I guess she wasn't able to make it. Something must have come up."

Verna clasped her hands at her bosom, her expression suddenly as solemn as a preacher's. "Yes, of course, something came up."

"And we all know what it was," the woman behind Helen whispered, though her cohort cut off any further remarks with another vivid "Hush!"

Unshaken, Helen looked straight ahead at Verna. "Jean's trying very hard to get this thing off the ground. She's calling it The Catery. Seeing how she's from River Bend, I say we give her a chance. It's the least we can do."

Verna pursed her lips, but she seemed to be considering the idea. "How about if we take a quick little vote?" she asked.

"Sounds fair enough," Helen said and plunked down in her chair.

"A show of hands, ladies?" their pink-clad president requested. "All in favor of having Jean Duncan cater the luncheon this year?"

Helen raised her arm quickly then turned this way and that to watch who followed suit. She had to bite her cheek to fight her grin when she saw a sea of hands fill the air.

"All opposed?"

Helen counted only half a dozen who didn't want to give Jean a shot, the blonde who'd supported the Catfish Barn among them.

"All right," Verna called out, "it's settled then. It looks like the job belongs to Jean." She nodded at Helen, who found it hard to sit still. "Would you mind giving her the news?"

"I'd love to." Jean would be thrilled, she knew, and it might be precisely the thing to take her mind off her estranged mother-in-law's sudden passing.

"Good. That's settled anyway." Verna shifted through the papers on the podium, the business of catering forgotten. "Let's move on to table linens, shall we? Last time, I think, we narrowed it down to yellow or blue. Ladies?"

But Helen heard little of what was said next. She was thinking of Jean, of how pleased she'd be at the turn of events. Maybe this would be the fresh start that she needed. After all her troubles these past two years, she certainly had it coming.

When the meeting finally ended about forty-five minutes later, Helen managed to slip away from the groups of women who hung around afterward to chat. Anxious to get over to Jean's, she headed off on foot, up the block and then across Main. She'd barely stepped off the curb when she heard a familiar voice behind her.

"Yoo hoo, Helen! Hey, wait up."

She paused in the gutter, looking over her shoulder to see Doc's wife coming after her. Fanny Melville pumped her arms as she walked, the skirt she wore dipping down to ankles bound by bobby socks. White Tretorns slapped the sidewalk underfoot. She was panting lightly when she caught up to Helen, but, after a few deep breaths, she tipped her chin and peered over her bifocals. "Always in the thick of things, aren't you?" Fanny said, not sounding winded in the least.

"I'm not sure I know what you're talking about," Helen replied.

"Oh, yes, you do," Fanny cut her off. "Amos says you were at Eleanora's last night just after Zelma found her body," she went on, her eyes bright.

Helen stepped back onto the curb so she and Fanny Melville stood on equal footing. "I happened to be there in the diner when Zelma came looking for the sheriff. If Eleanora was hurt, well, I wanted to help. But it seems we were all just a few minutes too late."

Below the white fringe of her bangs, Fanny's pale gaze dimmed. She shook her head. "It's awful, isn't it? Amos feels terrible about how things turned out. He said that if Zelma had just called him when Eleanora first started complaining, he might've been able to save her."

"Don't let Zelma hear you say that," Helen said. "It's likely to kill her. She was devoted to Eleanora."

"Hard to imagine anyone felt that way about the old girl," Doc's wife remarked, clicking tongue against teeth. "She was a prickly pear, wasn't she? I don't mean to speak ill of the dead, but she was a bitter lady. The way she treated poor Jean . . . " Her voice trailed off, and she sighed sympathetically.

Helen tried to change the subject. "Did Doc mention how soon the autopsy might be finished?"

"I imagine it shouldn't be long. Amos says Ed Drake told him they've had a real slow week at the morgue, so they could start on Eleanora first thing."

"What's he looking for, do you know?" Helen pressed, as Doc usually confided in Fanny, and Fanny in turn confided in just about anyone willing to listen.

"Well, of course, he has to consider the usual," Fanny

replied as she ticked off on her fingers, "heart attack, stroke, embolism, aneurysm, some type of allergy that proved fatal."

"And?" Helen knew those answers were merely the carrot meant to tease.

"And what?" Fanny raised her eyebrows. "Oh, you must mean what he thinks the toxicology results will show."

Helen's mouth went dry. "Does he think she was poisoned?"

"It's a possibility."

"Oh, my," Helen squeaked, her voice suddenly small. That was the reason Eleanora's fridge had practically been emptied out, along with the biscuits and whatever else it was Eleanora had been snacking on while Zelma had fixed dinner. Helen had assumed they'd leave no stone unturned, but to actually hear point-blank that they were checking for poisons sent a shiver up her spine. "Oh, dear," she murmured, "oh, dear."

"You can say that again."

"I hope Doc's wrong about that."

"All I can tell you is he's not counting anything out, though it's hard to imagine anyone would actually stoop to murdering the old girl. Eleanora might've been a tyrant, but to kill her?" Fanny exhaled slowly. "It's not like she hadn't made herself some enemies, Jean included."

"Fanny, please." Helen let out a noise of exasperation. "That's absurd," she said, amazed that Doc's wife would even intimate Jean might have had something to do with Eleanora's death. "Look, I've got to run. I want to give Jean the good news about the luncheon."

"Oh, sure, honey, go right along."

"Will you, um, let me know when Amos hears anything?"

Fanny smiled.

Helen started off across Main Street, following the zebra stripes of the crosswalk.

"Oh, wait, Helen?"

She paused in the middle of the road and turned around.

"Is bridge still on?" Fanny yelled.

"So far as I know," Helen called back, giving a little wave as she hurried off, thinking that her bridge group would have her head if she cancelled the weekly game for any reason other than murder. And even that was pretty iffy.

Chapter 7

HELEN PAUSED AT the base of Jean's driveway and stared up at the house.

The curtains were still closed behind the windows. Near Helen's feet lay a rolled-up morning newspaper. A glance at her watch told her it was half past eleven. Was Jean not yet up?

Helen bent to fetch the log of newsprint and walked up the driveway to the kitchen door. It was usually left open, the screen door unlatched.

But today it was closed and—Helen tried the knob—locked.

She shifted the paper to the crook of her arm and knocked, calling, "Jean? Hello? Is anyone home?"

When no one answered, Helen gave up, setting the newspaper down on the stoop. She walked around to the garage and peered through the dusty windows, but there was no sign of Jean's car.

Helen sighed, disappointed she'd have to wait to tell her friend about the catering job, but it appeared she'd have no choice in the matter.

She headed up the sidewalk, back toward Main Street. Then she hesitated at the fork where Harbor Drive veered left.

She was so close to the Duncan home, and she was certainly not in a hurry. It wouldn't hurt to check on Zelma, she decided. See how she was holding up.

The sun had risen above the bluffs and cast its warmth upon her shoulders, its rays undimmed by even the faintest wisps of clouds.

The river was so near that its muddy smell filled her nose. She could hear the occasional rush of a car or thunder of a truck upon the River Road that ran alongside the brown waters, but otherwise, save for the birds overhead, the day was blissfully calm.

She passed the harbor, where moored boats bobbed about like ducks, and spotted a pair of men with fishing rods on the docks.

A smile slipped across her mouth as she thought of those afternoons years ago when she and Joe had spent endless hours trying to hook a couple of catfish to fry for supper. Back when you could eat the darned things and it wouldn't kill you. Now fishing in the Mississippi was mostly for sport, and the only catfish she ate were pond-raised.

She shook her head as she walked, her smile disappearing as she thought what a damned shame it was. No wonder folks like that Floyd Baskin were up in arms.

She couldn't fault the man for his drive to save the river, though sometimes she questioned his means. Having his group dress up like dead fish and sprawl across the highway? It's a wonder, she thought, that no one had been run over by a motorist. Dyeing the community pool red in a symbolic gesture? *That* had certainly been a mess. The pool had needed to be drained, scrubbed, repainted, and re-filled, which had not endeared Mr. Baskin to many. His latest scandal had earned him some jail time, she'd heard, though it had gotten him plenty of press as well. The smoke bombs he'd set off at the power company down-river had activated the sprinkler systems and damaged a number of computers and equipment. She could still recall seeing Mr. Baskin on the nightly news as he was being dragged off to the paddy wagon. "This is just the beginning!" he'd yelled into the camera, his bearded face purple. "You ain't seen nothing yet, people, and I won't stop till something's done!"

Why, she wondered, did it even have to come to this, with fanatics like Baskin commandeering causes that, in the best of all worlds, wouldn't need to exist.

When she was young, no one worried about things like sewage and chemicals and toxic waste. And maybe that was part of the problem. No one considered the future, and what kind of life they were leaving for their grand-children. She was glad she wasn't growing up today, when it seemed everything you breathed or drank or ate was po-tentially fatal.

The sharp snapping of hedge clippers cut into her thoughts and she slowed her steps, glancing up to see a lone gardener at work on the rose bushes in a yard many times the size of her own.

With a quick tug on her sweatshirt, she started up the driveway that curved before the Duncan house, squinting at the sight of an older-model Lincoln parked at the base of the steps leading up to the porch.

She made her way around the mud-splattered car, climbing onto the portico. She patted her hair, smoothing it as best she could, then reached up to take hold of the brass knocker. The door came open at her touch.

Poking her head in, she called out, "Zelma, dear? It's me. Helen Evans."

She stepped into the foyer, finding herself walking nearly on tiptoe, feeling like a trespasser. "Zelma?"

She knew the housekeeper was rather hard of hearing, so she made her way into the kitchen.

Empty.

She headed down the rear hallway, perking up when she heard voices coming from the library. Raised voices.

"Zelma," she started to say, "is everything all . . . "

She paused in the doorway, her mouth hanging open.

"Good heavens," she breathed, surveying the papers scattered across the woven rug. The desk drawers had been turned upside down, the contents dumped on the floor. "What's going on here?"

Two faces turned her way.

Despite the thickness of the glasses distorting Zelma's eyes, Helen could tell she was near to tears.

The man apparently responsible for the mess scowled at Helen from across the room. Thin with salt-and-pepper hair, he had thick eyebrows slanted low over narrowed eyes that were anything but friendly.

"Oh, Mrs. Evans," Zelma cried, her hands clutching the front of her apron. "I tried to make him stop, but he wouldn't listen. Look what he's done to this place! Jesus, Joseph, and Mary, but Miss Nora will be furious . . ."

"She's dead, you old goat," the man snapped at her, and Zelma's face became even more pinched.

"She's dead," the housekeeper repeated, her owlish gaze suddenly downcast. "I'd forgotten for a minute."

The man merely sniffed and tugged out the one remaining desk drawer. Without concern that he was being watched, he went through it piece by piece, tossing papers to the floor just as quickly.

Helen looked at Zelma and then at the man who ignored her still. She clenched her hands into fists and picked her way across the littered rug, stopping on the other side of the desk. When he didn't look up, she pushed aside a jumble of papers to find the telephone. She lifted the receiver. "If you don't get out on the count of three," she told him, "I'll have no choice but to call Sheriff Biddle."

He glanced up at her and grunted, then went back to his rummaging.

"One," Helen said.

He didn't even look up.

"Two."

No reaction then either.

"Three," Helen said and started to dial.

The phone was snatched from her hand before she'd finished, the receiver clamped down with a clatter.

The man glared at her. "Good Lord, woman, you can't really call the police. I have a perfect right to be here. I'm a relative."

Helen turned to Zelma, who nodded rather unhappily.

"He's Mr. Duncan's brother," she explained, hands still kneading her apron.

"His baby brother," the man spoke up, rubbing his palms on the front of linen pants that looked rather threadbare. The faded blue polo shirt he wore had also seen better days. He had the air about him of someone who demanded more of life than he gave; there were lines about his eyes and mouth that she'd wager had more to do with age and less to do with hard work. He might have been about sixty-five, but it was difficult to tell. He certainly kept himself in good shape.

"Stanley Duncan," he said and extended his hand, which Helen made no move to take. He drew it back with a frown. "So now you're one up on me, aren't you? You know who I am, but I've no idea who you are. Perhaps," he intoned, "I'm the one who should be phoning the sheriff. You did just walk into the house uninvited, after all. I think that's called breaking and entering."

Why, the nerve of him! Helen fumed, when he'd torn up the library so that it looked like a tornado had weaved a path through it. She opened her mouth to sputter a retort but pressed it shut again.

Ah, yes, Stanley Duncan, Marvin's little brother. The name suddenly rang a bell. She'd heard Eleanora speak of him once or twice in no great detail. All Helen did recall were phrases like "deadbeat," "parasite," and "sponge."

He'd left River Bend years and years ago, not long after Helen and Joe had moved into the house at Jersey and Springfield. Though he might have dropped into town sporadically since, she'd never met him face-to-face until now.

Helen went to Zelma's side and put an arm around her. The housekeeper sagged against her shoulder. "I've come to see Zelma," she said, "although why you're here is a different story. What are you looking for, Mr. Duncan?" she pressed.

"As if that's any of your business," he snapped, returning his attention to the near-empty drawer.

Zelma was less cryptic. "He says he wants what belongs to him. He's after her money, I'm sure of it. He was always calling Miss Nora, demanding cash, ever since he spent whatever Mr. Marvin left him. Miss Nora helped him out at first. She'd send him a check so he'd leave her in peace. But she was through," Zelma stated and lifted her chin. "'The bank's closed,' that's what she told me to tell him when he came by yesterday afternoon."

"Shut up, you old bat!" Stanley tossed the drawer to the floor with a clunk, the noise enough to make Zelma cower.

The hair at Helen's nape bristled. "If you're expecting some money from Eleanora, Mr. Duncan, I'd suggest you wait until her will's read, though it may be a few days. Her cause of death has to be determined before the certificate can be signed, so everything's all neat and legal."

"I don't care how she died or even that she's dead!" he shouted, his clean-shaven face turning ruddy. Helen might have found him handsome if she hadn't glimpsed the ugliness of his character. "All I want is what's mine, you got that? And I won't leave until I find it!"

"Heaven help me," Zelma breathed.

Helen had heard enough. She let go of the housekeeper and stomped toward Stanley, this time disregarding the papers that crackled under her feet. "All right, Mr. Duncan, you've had your fun. But now it's over. Either you take yourself out of the house right this moment, or I will most certainly call the sheriff, no matter if I have to use another phone to do it!"

Take that, buddy!

She crossed her arms and planted herself, standing as tall as her five feet and five inches would allow. Though she barely reached Stanley's chin, he seemed to get the message that she meant business, and she strongly doubted that he'd relish tangling with the law.

He raised his hands. "Okay, you win. I'll go." He looked past her at Zelma and shook a finger. "But I'll be back. I'm not leaving town till I get what's mine, you understand?" His eyes settled on Helen again. "As far as the will goes, I guess I'll be hearing from her lawyers sometime soon enough. I'm the only surviving Duncan, so maybe I'll finally get back everything that should've been mine when Marv died. He meant for me to have more than the few bucks I got, I know he did. It was that old battle-axe he married who made sure I was cut out."

With that said, he spun on a heel and left.

Helen followed to make sure he was really gone; she didn't feel satisfied until she stood on the porch and watched his dusty Lincoln drive away.

Zelma came up behind her. "Miss Nora always said Mr. Stanley was spoiled something awful when he was a baby, being that he was so much younger. She said he never did get over it."

"Eleanora was right."

Zelma sighed. "Miss Nora knew how to take care of him. She wasn't afraid of him in the least."

Helen looked into the tired face. "And you are, aren't you, dear?"

Zelma didn't answer. Instead, she brushed her trembling hands against her apron, hung her head, and shuffled inside.

Chapter 8

THE SCREEN DOOR squealed open then slapped shut again.

Frank Biddle looked up from the *Alton Telegraph* spread on his desk. When he saw Amos Melville, he quickly folded the paper and stuffed it away in his top drawer.

"How do, Sheriff."

"Something up, Doc?" Frank checked his watch. "You on your lunch break already?"

"Just between appointments," Amos told him, and Frank nodded.

The sheriff knew that many folks in River Bend, like Amos Melville, still worked nine to five despite being past the usual retirement age. It heartened a middle-aged man like Frank to see all the gray hairs that kept things humming on Main Street, like Erma serving food at the diner, Hilary Dell running the stationery store, and Agnes March selling antiques just next door. People didn't stop *doing* in this town just because they passed sixty-five.

There were no big corporate bullies to tell them when they should retire, so it seemed to Frank that few did. Though he didn't wager he'd be sheriff too far into his sunset years, it gave him a good feeling to know that no one around here would even blink if he wore his badge for another decade or more.

With an overloud sigh, Doc settled into the chair opposite his desk.

Uh-oh, Frank thought and cleared his throat. He had a feeling this wasn't just a friendly visit. "You've heard from your friend at the medical examiner's office," he said as much as asked.

Amos ran a hand over his fluff of white hair, pushing back the strands that had fallen over his brow. He stuck his bifocals onto his crown and rubbed his eyes as he spoke. "Some of the tests have been run, and it doesn't look good."

"I see." Biddle couldn't think of any other comment. So he listened.

"There's evidence of hemorrhagic gastroenteritis, which is inflammation and bleeding of the stomach and intestines," Doc clarified, propping his specs back on his nose. "Ed found signs of cerebral edema and central nervous system depression, enough to have caused complete respiratory failure."

Biddle cleared his throat. "Which in plain English means what?"

"It looks like Eleanora was poisoned."

Biddle leaned forward. "Any sign of what did it?" he asked.

Doc's pale eyes met his. "The tests of her organs and tissue aren't all in yet. But from what's been done so far and from the symptoms of tremor and convulsion Zelma described, I'd wager it was some kind of acid or acid compound, though I'd hate to trap myself into a guess just yet. The lab will narrow down an answer soon enough."

"Poisoned." Biddle breathed the word, dropping his hands to his knees and slumping back in his chair. "So someone did kill old Mrs. Duncan."

"I'm afraid so."

"Ingested?"

Doc nodded.

"Think it was in the food she was snacking on while Zelma fixed her dinner?"

"Ed said he'd have all the answers later on this afternoon."

"Holy cow," Biddle murmured, his chair squealing as he rocked forward again and got to his feet. He hiked up his pants, though his belly kept them from budging much higher. "I can't believe someone really did her in." He shook his head and turned on his heel so he was looking down at Doc. "You're sure about this, now?"

"I'm dead certain."

Frank raised his brows.

Doc tacked on, "So to speak."

"She was murdered," Frank said, simply because it floored him each time something like that happened in this tiny town. For the most part, major crimes involved fishing rods stolen from boats in the harbor or skinny-dipping in the community pool on hot summer nights.

"Murdered," he repeated, more softly this time, thinking of the car that had tried to run down Eleanora Duncan the previous morning. Were the two incidents connected? He had suggested as much last night, but it had been a comment made on the spur of the moment. Now he wasn't so certain he hadn't been right.

Doc came out of his chair. "I'd better run. Fanny's got a kid coming in with chicken pox in half an hour. Think I'll pick up a sandwich at the diner and take it back to my desk."

"Holler when you know something more," Frank called as Doc left his office.

The sheriff got up and walked over to the screen door. He looked through the mesh, watching as Amos Melville crossed Main Street and headed straight for the diner. Every now and again, a car would creep its way up the street or down. Voices cropped up and faded as people passed his office at a leisurely pace. No one in River Bend ever seemed in much of a hurry. Frank figured that was part of why he liked it here.

He'd left the police force in St. Charles a number of years ago, settling into this tiny river-side community with Sarah and running for sheriff unopposed. He'd gotten tired of the crime that had seemed to spread like a fungus beyond the St. Louis metroplex, creeping into St. Charles. He'd wanted something better for himself and Sarah. He'd figured River Bend was the answer, particularly since he didn't like using a gun. Most of the time he could get through a week without anything more urgent than calls about cats up in trees or a fender bender on the graveled roads. Once in a while, some kid would pocket a candy bar or a magazine from the drugstore or steal a pickup and go joyriding up to Cemetery Hill.

But murder?

That wasn't something he saw much of in River Bend. With so many older folks in town, death wasn't uncommon. But dying in your sleep wasn't criminal. Eleanora Duncan hadn't gone willingly. Someone had given her a shove.

Biddle sighed again.

Now all he had to do was figure out who did it.

His stomach grumbled, and he realized he was hungry.

He couldn't do much on the Duncan case until the medical examiner had finished the autopsy, so he figured he might as well have lunch.

He pushed open the screen door and went out. He let the door slap shut behind him. Hiking up his pants, he started across the street as Doc Melville had a minute before, making a beeline toward the diner just as the carillon in the chapel began to play a noontime tune.

Chapter 9

THE PLUCKY CHIMES of the carillon filled the air as Helen walked home from the Duncan house.

Without so much as a glance at her wristwatch, she knew it was noon. Her stomach growled on cue, and she wondered if somehow her body hadn't over the years learned to react to the carillon's chimes at midday and dusk like Pavlov's dog.

As she approached her cottage, she noticed that the screen door had been pushed open about six inches. Helen figured that Amber had made his way inside, ready for lunch. That was all well and good so long as the old tom hadn't brought her anything from the creek bed or the bluffs, like a frog or the little gray field mice he was so fond of.

She entered the house and surveyed the porch. Carefully, she inspected the floral cushions atop the white wicker. She even stooped to check beneath the sofa and chairs, but she didn't see anything more startling than dust bunnies.

Entering the interior through open French doors, Helen crossed the dining room and went into the kitchen.

There he was, as expected.

Amber sat on the floor with his tail vaguely twitching. His ears pricked up at her footsteps, but otherwise he gave no indication that he was happy to see her.

He stared sadly down at his food bowl, which Helen had filled with Salmon 'n' Cod just that morning and which now appeared nearly empty. Whatever did he find so engrossing about his leftover breakfast?

"You're not old enough to be senile," she murmured, taking a few steps closer. Despite how her knees protested, she crouched low behind him and squinted down at the linoleum. Within seconds, she saw what caught his interest.

A thin trail of black ants marched from a crack in the floorboard below the dishwasher across to Amber's saucer and back again.

"Ugh," she muttered and slowly straightened, putting her hands on her hips. She looked down at Amber, who turned his yellow eyes in her direction. "Well," she told him, "*do* something, would you? Earn your rent."

He blinked at her, and his pink-gummed mouth seemed to be grinning, as though he was enjoying the whole scene immensely.

Helen sighed, realizing she was going to have to take care of the ant trail herself. She lifted a sneakered foot and brought it down, squashing as many of the little buggers as she could. With a grimace, she scratched their carcasses off the sole of her Ked with a paper towel.

Amber mewed gruffly, like she'd spoiled his fun. Then he sauntered off with his tail in the air.

"Sorry, pal," Helen said as he disappeared around the corner. Gathering up her courage, she pulled open the dishwasher but didn't see a sign of ants inside. Well, that was something good, anyway.

Though she scrounged beneath the sink, pushing aside cans of air freshener, floor cleaner, spot remover, brass and silver polish, and assorted other sparklers and shiners she didn't use near as much as she should, all Helen could find was a bottle of ant killer with just about a drop left. Definitely not enough to do the job at hand. Splat, it was called, and it was great stuff. Made by a little company in St. Louis, it got rid of the pests better than any big-name brand she'd ever tried. She'd heard talk it was about to be banned—but then Helen heard lots of talk around here—and besides, the corner market still stocked it. Helen knew she wasn't the only one who'd raise a stink if she couldn't buy some. It was the one thing that truly worked against modern-day bugs with their cast-iron stomachs.

She dusted off her hands and dropped the empty bottle of Splat into the trash can.

Hmm, she thought as she peered into her near-empty refrigerator; if she didn't get to the grocer's pretty soon, even the ants wouldn't have much to snack on. She knew her stash of cat food for Amber *was* getting dangerously low. All right, all right. After she put something in her stomach, she'd take a trip to the store and fill up.

That settled, she gathered up the few slices of American cheese, butter, and bread that remained and fixed herself a grilled cheese sandwich. It was exactly what she'd meant to eat for supper the night before but had forsaken when Jean had called and asked to meet her at the diner. What with dogging Frank Biddle to Eleanora's and finding her dead, Helen had ended up coming home to a bowl of Raisin Bran at close to nine o'clock.

She took the sandwich and a glass of ice water out onto the porch. Within five minutes, she'd devoured the grilled cheese, even licking the greasy residue off her fingertips when she was done.

It took her twice as long to locate her glasses. When she found them buried behind seat cushions on the wicker couch, she propped them on her nose and retrieved that morning's *Alton Telegraph*. She neatly folded the paper to the section that featured the crossword puzzle. The purple pen she used to fill in the squares sat right beside it. She picked both up and settled down.

Ten across. Five letters.

A river in German wine country (Ger. sp.).

Helen paused for a moment, but only that, then said aloud, "Mosel," writing down the answer in deep lavender print.

She backtracked to three down.

A seven-letter word for insolent.

"Stanley," she uttered without thinking, laughing at herself when she realized what she'd said. Well, it fit, didn't it? And Stanley Duncan certainly was insolent if nothing else.

It was too bad, she mused, as she filled in the squares with "abusive," that Eleanora couldn't have used a little Splat to rid herself of her awful brother-in-law.

What gall he had, tearing through Eleanora's things like a madman, frightening Zelma half to death, and with Eleanora not even buried.

She found herself hoping Eleanora had left the obnoxious man little, if anything, in her will. Unfortunately, she realized, he *was* the only Duncan left, the only surviving family.

Poor Eleanora, she thought. What else had the woman had to put up with that Helen hadn't known about? Who else besides Stanley Duncan had wanted something from the old girl?

Stop it, she told herself. Eleanora wouldn't want your pity.

Still, Helen suddenly wasn't in the mood to do any more of her crossword. She set down the paper and pen alongside her spectacles then cleared her dishes from the porch. After putting her dirty plate and glass in the sink, she gathered up her purse and headed off for the corner market.

Just as Helen was approaching the doors leading into the store, she ran smack into Jemima Winthrop, who rushed out like the place was on fire.

"My, but you're in a hurry," Helen said, rubbing her arm where Jemima had bumped it.

Jemima mumbled an apology but didn't pause. She

tightly clutched the small brown sack in her hands and dashed off.

Helen watched her go, striding away up the sidewalk in her khaki pants and pale sweater, shoulders stiff and back ramrod straight. Jemima was much like her father had been, feisty and determined, quick to speak and as quick to act. The family had once held a fortune nearly as big as the Duncans' before there had been some sort of trouble, and Reginald Winthrop had ended up practically giving away his granary to Marvin Duncan in some type of bankruptcy auction. Old Mr. Winthrop had taken to drinking and had died not long after, leaving behind his wife and unmarried daughter. Jemima, headstrong girl that she was, had plunged into volunteer work, taking over the reins of the local library, doing her damnedest to make it something to be proud of.

Maybe she had urgent library business that had sent her scurrying off. Certainly Jemima hadn't meant to give her the brush-off? Helen shrugged. No matter, she thought and shoved open the glass door to the market.

Half an hour later, she pushed her cart up to the counter, unloading her goodies one by one so the ponytailed checkout girl could ring her up.

A display of Splat near the register reminded Helen she was out of the stuff, and she quickly added a bottle to the rest.

"Ants must be bad this year," the teenager said, noting the purchase. "'Cause I've sold, like, a hundred bottles of the stuff this week alone. Miss Winthrop just bought her second batch in two days, would you believe."

"All I know is I've got an army of ants in my kitchen," Helen told her, writing a check for the total as the girl packed the groceries into two recyclable bags.

"Good luck with the Splat," the checker said, waving as Helen left.

By the time she'd walked home, Helen's arms were dead tired. She'd barely set the bags down on the kitchen counter when the phone shrilly rang. She hurried to catch it. Whatever happened to that nice jingly-ring landlines used to have? she wondered as she scooped up the receiver and uttered a brisk "Hello?"

"Helen, it's Jean," said the excited voice on the other end.

"Jean? For goodness' sake, where've you been?" Helen started in. "I've been trying to reach you since last evening. I've left several messages on your voice mail. I even went by your place this morning after the LCIL meeting, but you weren't around." She paused to take a breath, which allowed Jean to jump in and explain.

"Did you leave a message? I haven't checked them yet. I had to go into St. Louis late last night and ended up staying with a friend. You won't believe what's happened . . . "

"No, dear, I think it's you who'll be surprised to hear what's been going on."

"Listen, Helen . . . "

"No, *you* listen, my friend . . . "

Jean burst in before Helen could finish. "If you come over right now, I'll explain everything. Will you do it?"

"Of course," Helen told her. How could she refuse, when her curiosity was on overload? "Give me about half an hour," she said then hung up.

She got the groceries unpacked in record time. After a quick pit stop, she was off, heading back toward Bluff Street, thinking that all of this walking would no doubt mean going to sleep tonight with her nose filled with the smell of Bengay.

Jean came out of the house as soon as Helen turned into the driveway.

"I've got wonderful news," Jean said as she took Helen's arm and walked with her up to the house. Jean's eyes were bright, her cheeks flushed. She looked every bit as excited as she'd sounded on the phone. "Something good has finally happened to me, and it's about time, don't you think?"

"Jean, wait." Helen stopped walking.

Jean let go of her arm and stared at her, puzzled. "Whatever's the matter with you? You're acting as if I've done something wrong."

"You *did* hear about Eleanora?"

Jean's sunny face clouded. "I told you last night that I don't want to have a thing to do with her anymore. So if you've got some sob story about her falling and breaking a hip, I don't want to hear it, not even after Zelma's histrionics in the diner last night."

"Oh, I think you might," Helen insisted.

"You make it sound serious. Should I sit down for this?"

"That's not a bad idea."

Jean nodded and went over to the steps, settling on the stoop. "Okay, shoot," she said once she was off her feet.

Helen went to sit beside her. "All right, here goes," she said and dove right in. "Eleanora's dead." There was no easy way to put it. "She was having convulsions then stopped breathing. That's why Zelma came after the sheriff. By the time help arrived, it was too late. I'm sorry."

Jean set her arms across her knees and looked away. "Well, she was nearly eighty-one. She had to go sometime."

Helen stared at her, speechless for once in her life. Such a coldhearted reply wasn't like the Jean Duncan she knew at all. But then, Eleanora had hardly been a loving mother-in-law to the woman. Still, she'd expected shock or sympathy, *something* more than this. Instead, she heard only indifference.

She studied Jean's profile and saw no softness; just the hard set of her jaw and the frown on her mouth. "Aren't you even the least bit curious as to *how* she died?" Helen quietly asked.

Jean replied with a cool "No, I can't say that I am."

"It so happens they took her body to the morgue for . . . "

"Helen, stop," Jean said and got to her feet. "I don't want to talk about Eleanora, not now or ever." She offered Helen her hand. "Now, do you want to come inside and have some coffee so I can fill you in on my first official job as a caterer?"

Helen realized that pursuing the subject of Eleanora Duncan was fighting a losing battle. "All right, you win." She got up and brushed off the back of her sweatpants.

Jean pulled the screen door wide, waving an arm. "After you," she said, and her eyes lit up again. She smiled brightly, as though Helen had never even made mention of Eleanora's death.

Helen stepped into the kitchen and sat at a table cluttered with cookbooks and handwritten recipe cards.

Jean poured them each a mug of coffee smelling deliciously of cinnamon. She passed Helen's over then pulled out the chair beside Helen's.

"Hmm, were should I start?" she said, rubbing her hands together. "Okay, last night after you left me stranded at the diner, I had Erma pack me up a meat loaf sandwich and brought it home. The phone was ringing just as I walked in. Turns out it was a friend of mine from college who'd moved to St. Louis about a week before and looked me up. Seems she's with a public relations firm that's putting on a fancy brouhaha for some clients, and their caterer bailed at the last minute. She said the company was in a panic, and did I know any good people, since she was new to the city and all. When I mentioned I'd started up a catering business myself, she asked if I'd consider working their party. Only thing was, they had to hire someone by this morning. So I hightailed it over to her place and spent most of the night working on menus and bouncing ideas off her until I had something really good put together."

"Does that mean you got the job?" Helen asked while Jean drew in a much needed breath.

"Yes!" Her scarf-tied ponytail swayed as she announced with a squeal, "I got it, Helen! I went into work with her this morning, showed them my stuff, and they told me the job was mine. Can you even believe it? I'm still on cloud nine."

Helen hardly knew what to say.

"Well? Aren't you going to congratulate me?"

"Of course I am. Congratulations," Helen said and reached for her hand, squeezing it warmly. She summoned up a smile, genuinely glad for her friend. "I'm thrilled," she said. "And you do deserve it. This past year's been so hard."

"I'm determined to put it behind me."

"When's this party? I only hope it won't interfere with the LCIL luncheon."

"Oh, my God, the luncheon," Jean repeated, and she raised her eyebrows. "Oh, Helen, don't tell me that I got the gig?" Her hands went to her heart. "Is it possible?"

"The gig is yours," Helen said, grinning, tickled by the look of surprise on Jean's face. "Well, it's yours if you want it."

Jean breathed a soft "Oh, my."

Helen took a sip of coffee, glad she set the cup down when she did, or it would've splattered across her sweatshirt when Jean hopped out of her chair and caught her in a hug.

"You did it, didn't you? Probably forced me down their throats," she was saying. "I can't thank you enough."

Helen laughed. "For heaven's sake, I was doing myself a favor. I couldn't bear the thought of having the Catfish Barn cater again this year. My intestines would never forgive me."

The doorbell rang, and Jean let Helen go. Jean straightened up, tucking her blouse tighter inside her blue jeans.

"Are you expecting someone?" Helen asked.

Jean shrugged. "Not that I'm aware of."

The bell chimed again.

"I'm coming!" Jean shouted. Assuring Helen she'd be

back in a flash, she left the kitchen, the tap of her flat-soled shoes audible even after she was out of sight.

Helen listened as the front door opened and she heard a man's voice, one she recognized well.

She got out of her chair and retraced Jean's steps, walking into the foyer to see Frank Biddle standing in the doorway, his hat in his hands.

Jean turned to her with cheeks pale as chalk. "Oh, God, Helen," she said, a warble in her voice. "Why didn't you tell me the whole story? Eleanora didn't just *die*, she was murdered."

Chapter 10

"ELEANORA WAS MURDERED?" Helen repeated, walking up to Jean and taking her arm. Her friend looked like she might faint. Helen didn't feel very steady on her feet either. "So it's for certain then? It wasn't natural causes?"

"No, ma'am, it was poison," Biddle told them. He spun his hat round and round in his hands. He didn't seem any more at ease with the answer than she or Jean. "Doc said it was sodium tetraborate."

"Oh, no," Jean breathed and swayed against Helen, who kept an arm around her waist to steady her. "Oh, no, this can't be happening."

"Sodium tetra . . . what?" Helen asked the sheriff. Her chest tightened at the thought of such violence in River Bend, of all places.

"Sodium tetraborate," Frank Biddle repeated, enunciating each syllable. "It's a form of boric acid." He glanced at Helen then Jean and back again. "It's mostly used in insecticides."

"Are you sure it was intentional?" Helen asked, wondering if the sheriff and Jean could hear the overloud beat of her heart. Her ears pounded with the noise of it. "Maybe it was an accident." At Biddle's lift of eyebrows, she added, "It has been known to happen."

"The evidence is pretty forthright, ma'am." The sheriff cleared his throat and inclined his head toward Jean, who stared at the floor, eyes unblinking, as though in shock. "Forensics tested what remained of the goose liver old Mrs. Duncan had been eating, and, from the concentration in what was left, they figured there was probably at least a teaspoon mixed in. It was more than enough to kill someone. It's relatively odorless, you know. Doc said that since our senses dull with age, she probably didn't even taste it."

Helen nodded. Her mouth was too dry to form words. She found herself thinking of the car that had nearly hit Eleanora yesterday morning and wondered if the person behind the wheel had been the one to put poison in the goose liver. Suddenly she didn't feel at all well.

Oh, boy.

She wet her lips and forced herself to ask, "This goose liver that had poison, was it something that . . ."

That Jean had delivered earlier that same day, she left unfinished.

"It was in a plastic deli-type dish with a lid that had The Catery printed on it," the sheriff answered. "It had Mrs. Duncan's phone number and website, too. *This* Mrs. Duncan," he added, nodding at Jean. "As I explained to her a moment ago, that's the reason I'm here. I need to ask her some questions."

"But, Sheriff, I had nothing to do with it." Jean eyes were as wide as a child's. "I-I didn't put p-poison in the pâté," she stammered and gestured helplessly. "You can't believe it was me? But you must, or you wouldn't have shown up on my doorstep."

"Ma'am, I just . . . "

"Really, Sheriff, you can't honestly think Jean killed her own mother-in-law," Helen butted in, still digesting the fact that Eleanora had been murdered and it was Jean's goose liver that had done her in. She stared at Frank Biddle in his tan uniform, his brown tie stained with ketchup. Through the open door beyond his shoulder, she saw his black-and-white parked at the curb. "For heaven's sake, you haven't come to arrest her?" she asked, the severity of the whole situation sinking in.

"Oh, no," Jean murmured again, and Helen felt her sway.

The sheriff tucked his hat under his arm and shifted on his feet. "Look, I didn't come to arrest anyone. I just need to ask Mrs. Duncan some questions. So if you don't mind, Mrs. Evans, I'd like to talk to Jean," he said.

"Of course," Helen said and tightened her arm around Jean. "Come on, dear," she said, leading her out of the foyer.

"Um, where do you think you're going?" Biddle called after her.

Without missing a step, Helen tossed over her shoulder, "To the den, Sheriff. Are you coming or not?"

She heard the door as he closed—or, rather,

slammed—it and the clomp of his boots as he crossed the tiled floor.

Helen had Jean settled beside her on the chintz-covered sofa by the time he walked into the den and dropped his hat onto the glass-topped coffee table. He plunked down with a grunt into a nearby overstuffed chair.

"Would you like a glass of water?" Helen asked Jean, but her friend shook her head, telling Helen in a voice so soft that Helen had to strain to hear, "Don't leave me alone with him, please."

Helen patted her arm. "As long as you need me, I'll be here."

The sheriff loudly cleared his throat. "Do you mind, ma'am?" he said, and Helen glanced up to find his eyes on her. He pulled a small notepad from his shirt pocket, slipped a pencil from its spine, and flipped the cover back to reveal a blank page. "Okay if I start?"

Helen turned to Jean. "Are you sure you're up to this?"

Her friend answered with a quick jerk of her chin. She clasped her hands in her lap and held her jaw square. She seemed over the shock of hearing about Eleanora and more pulled together than Helen would have been.

"All right, Sheriff," Jean said, her voice remarkably steady. "What is it you want to know? Did I get along with my mother-in-law?" she started in before Biddle could speak up. "Well, the answer is no, though I'm sure I don't have to convince you. The whole town knows how Eleanora treated me since the accident." She hesitated, drawing in a sharp breath, though she didn't drop her guard, not an inch. "She was horrible to me, really horrible. But did I hate her enough to kill her?" Her chin fell, as did her voice. "Maybe I thought about it, maybe I wished her dead a few times, but"—she raised her eyes—"I didn't do it. I pitied her more than anything. She had lost all that was dear to her. I couldn't blame her for hardening her heart."

"The goose liver," Biddle said after scribbling furiously on his notepad, "how'd it end up with old Mrs. Duncan? When you didn't like her, I mean."

"Well, I can tell you that much, Sheriff," Helen interjected, leaning forward in her seat, but the sheriff waved his pencil in the air.

"I'd like to hear it from Mrs. Duncan, please."

Helen settled back against the cushion, frowning, feeling a bit like a child who'd been told to wait her turn.

Jean sighed. "I was whipping up some appetizers yesterday morning. Samples of hors d'oeuvres and dips that I could drop off around town with some of the women's groups and committees. Helen came around while I was making up the pâté."

"It's true, I did," Helen said and nodded, adding with unfettered sarcasm, "and I certainly never saw her add even a teaspoon of poison to anything."

Sheriff Biddle stopped writing. His mouth turned down. "That's all very interesting, Mrs. Evans, but if you could just keep quiet until I finish with Mrs. Duncan, I might have a few questions for you as well."

"I'm only trying to help—"

The sheriff cut her off. "Well, if you wouldn't mind not helping for another few minutes, I'd appreciate it, ma'am."

Helen didn't respond. She merely pressed her mouth tightly shut, though it wouldn't be easy to sit quietly through this, not when his questions all seemed to intimate that Jean was involved in Eleanora's death.

"Go on, Mrs. Duncan," Biddle coaxed. "You were saying you'd made some hors d'oeuvres."

Jean pursed her lips before explaining, "Helen mentioned that Eleanora felt shaken after nearly being hit by a car, and I felt guilty, thinking she might've been killed and with all this garbage between us. I don't know why exactly, but I wanted to see her. I figured I'd take some of my samples over as a gesture of goodwill." She toyed with her wedding band and sat in silence for a moment. "They say that a brush with death makes people appreciate life. I thought maybe she'd realize how silly she'd been, I don't know." She sighed before continuing. "Anyway, I went to the house yesterday afternoon."

Biddle had his tongue caught in the corner of his mouth as he jotted down Jean's remarks, flipping to an empty page as soon as he'd filled one. When he realized she'd stopped talking, he looked up. "And what happened then, ma'am? Once you saw old Mrs. Duncan?"

"Oh, I didn't actually *see* her, Sheriff."

The lines at Biddle's wide forehead deepened. "She wasn't home?"

"Yes, she was home," Jean told him. "That's why I never got past the kitchen." Her voice tight, she went on, "I guess when Zelma tracked down Eleanora and told her I was there, she received orders to send me packing."

"So you were in the kitchen alone, ma'am?"

Jean was slow to answer. "Yes, I was alone. But only for a minute or two."

"And after that?"

Jean shrugged. "When Zelma came back and asked me to leave on Eleanora's orders, I took off. I had a few other errands to run, and I met Helen at the diner at dusk. You were there, weren't you, Sheriff?"

Biddle glanced up from his notes. "Yes, ma'am, I was."

"I went into St. Louis afterward, and I didn't return until this morning," she said, keeping her tone level. "So I didn't even find out that Eleanora had passed until Helen came over a half hour ago."

"She was taken by surprise," Helen said, figuring she'd held still for long enough. She glanced at Jean, who avoided her eyes. "She didn't know a thing about how Eleanora died, and she didn't ask."

As he scribbled, the sheriff murmured, "Maybe that's because she already knew."

"Please," Helen sputtered.

Jean stood, her face flushed, the set of her mouth grim. "I think I've answered all your questions, Sheriff. So if you wouldn't mind showing yourself out, I have a business to run. Now if you'll excuse me," she said and escaped through the back hallway leading to the kitchen.

Helen didn't say a word till the *click-clack* of Jean's footsteps died away.

Then she slid over to the edge of the sofa, fixed her eyes on Frank Biddle, and scolded, "That was uncalled for, and you know it."

The sheriff didn't respond. He merely returned the tiny pencil to the notepad, flipped it closed, and tucked it into his pocket. He put his hands on his knees and gave Helen a stern look. "If you haven't realized it already, ma'am, this is a murder investigation, not a tea party."

"You practically accused her of Eleanora's murder!"

He picked up his hat from the table. "If she's guilty, Mrs. Evans, I'll find out. And even though you're her friend, you won't be able to protect her."

Helen felt her blood pressure rise. This so-called investigation wasn't going to be good for her health, she could tell that much already. "Jean didn't kill anyone," she told him, wondering why her voice didn't sound as convincing as it should. For goodness' sake, she didn't believe it for a moment.

"No," she said, for her own sake as much as Biddle's. "Jean wouldn't do such a thing. She couldn't." Something came to mind then, and she nearly laughed aloud. "Why, just yesterday as I was leaving here, after Jean had made up her mind to go to Eleanora's, she made a comment about hoping Eleanora wouldn't accuse her of trying to poison her." She smiled at the irony. "If that doesn't prove she's innocent, then I don't know what does. Why on earth would she say such a thing and then go poison her mother-in-law? That would be like pointing the finger at herself, wouldn't it?" She shook her head. "No, Sheriff. That would be way too foolish. And Jean's not a foolish woman."

"You're right, ma'am. She's not," he said dryly as he rose to his feet.

Helen got up, too.

He tugged on his hat. "Tell Mrs. Duncan I might need to talk to her again."

"I don't know why," Helen scoffed.

"Oh, and Mrs. Evans?" he asked from the doorway. "Don't let yourself get dragged into this one. It's not your concern." Then he tipped his head at her and left.

The heck it wasn't, Helen thought, feeling suddenly weak in the knees.

Chapter 11

FRANK BIDDLE STARTED up his car and pulled away from Jean Duncan's house, heading for Harbor Drive.

Why, he wondered, did Helen Evans seem to be everywhere at once?

She'd shown up at Eleanora Duncan's before the body was even cold. Then when he'd knocked on the daughter-in-law's door to ask her a few questions, Mrs. Evans had been there, too, with a protective arm around the younger Mrs. Duncan, endlessly interjecting and keeping him from doing his job.

He hit his hand on the steering wheel and grunted with frustration.

Did Helen Evans have a police scanner filed away in that gray head of hers? Whenever there was trouble in River Bend—and admittedly, it didn't happen too often—she always appeared in the thick of it. Didn't she have enough to keep her busy with nine grandkids plus all those women's committees and bridge groups she belonged to?

He had to say one thing about her though: age didn't slow her down. No wonder she ran around town in sweat suits and sneakers. Keeping her nose poked in so many other people's business probably gave her a good workout.

He let out a slow breath as he drove past the harbor and down the road lined with houses as grand as those in any big city.

As his tires crunched over graveled pavement, he pulled the car against the curb in front of the imposing Victorian belonging to Eleanora Duncan. Well, that *had* belonged to her, anyway.

Frank reminded himself to check that out with her attorney. He needed to find out who'd get the place, not to mention the rest of her assets, now that the old lady was gone.

He slapped the car door closed and rounded the hood, crossing under an overhanging oak and then up a cobblestone path flanked by budding pink flowers. He appreciated a nicely landscaped lawn, though he wasn't much of a green thumb himself. When he was off duty, the last thing he wanted to do was mow the grass or plant a bunch of pansies, though Sarah was always bugging him about pruning this tree or that.

Frank slogged up the stairs and stood on the porch, taking a look around him. Then he hiked up his pants, which promptly slipped back to the same spot on his hips below his protuberant belly—yet another thing Sarah was always nagging him about. These days it seemed like every other word she uttered seemed to be "fat" or "cholesterol."

With her out of town, no one told him what to eat and when. Erma at the diner merely asked him, "What'll it be?" and served it to him hot and quick.

He smiled to himself as he reached for the doorbell and pressed it soundly. He removed his hat, turning it around in his hands while he waited for someone to answer.

When no one came, he tried the brass knocker but got similar results. He touched the door handle and heard the latch click free. It was unlocked.

He pushed the door wide and ducked his head in. "Hello?" he called out. "Is anyone home? Miss Burdine, are you here?"

He heard the shuffle of footsteps a minute after. Sure enough, Zelma emerged from the rear hallway, hands kneading the hem of her apron.

"Sheriff Biddle," she said and stopped in her tracks. Her eyes blinked behind thick round frames. "Is anything wrong? Had you told me you were coming by this afternoon? I'm sorry, but I don't remember. My mind seems to be all in a fog what with everything that's gone on."

"No, ma'am, you wouldn't have been expecting me," he assured her as he made his way into the foyer. He dropped his hat onto a marble-topped table beside a stack of mail that Eleanora Duncan would never open. "It's just that the preliminary autopsy report's come in, and I have a few questions to ask you. You see, old Mrs. Duncan . . . I mean, your Miss Nora," he began unsuccessfully, tripping over his tongue. He didn't know any way to sugarcoat what he was about to say. "Well, ma'am, it appears she was poisoned."

Zelma twisted her apron. Her mouth fell open, but no words came out.

"Looks like she ate some goose liver that was full of sodium tetraborate," Frank informed her.

Zelma stared at him with that same blank stare. Her wrinkled face didn't even twitch beneath the cap of mousy hair.

The sheriff pressed on. "I know Jean Duncan was here the afternoon of the murder. She told me herself that she brought over some food she'd made. Did you put it into the refrigerator, or did she?"

Zelma finally found the voice to answer. "Oh, dear, I can't recall," she said and swallowed, the folds of her neck quivering. She pressed a finger to her chin. "Wait, I remember. Miss Jean stuck everything in the fridge herself while I went to the library to tell Miss Nora she was here." The housekeeper frowned. "Miss Nora didn't want to see her. She was very upset that I'd let Miss Jean into the house." Zelma rubbed her hands on the skirt of her apron. "Miss Nora didn't care much for Miss Jean, not after Miss Jean drove the car off the road and killed Jim."

Frank nodded. He'd heard the story before often enough. Sarah was a big one for gossip, so he pretty well knew all there was to know about most folks in town.

He looked across the foyer to the dining room on his right. It was chockfull of heavy furniture, probably pricey antiques. Above his head, an enormous crystal chandelier dripped from the recessed ceiling. Would Zelma inherit anything? he wondered. Whoever did get Eleanora Duncan's assets certainly wouldn't want for much.

"Ma'am," he said, fixing his attention back on Zelma Burdine, "is there somewhere we can sit down for a minute and talk?"

"Certainly, Sheriff," the older woman replied, bobbing her head. "Would you mind coming into the kitchen? I was about to feed the cat. She's supposed to eat at precisely twelve o'clock, and I'm late as it is."

"That'll be just fine, ma'am." He followed after her, walking slowly behind her shuffling gait.

Frank settled into a chair at the kitchen table and couldn't keep his gaze from wandering to the spot on the floor where he'd found Eleanora Duncan lying the night before. His stomach did a little flip-flop and he swallowed, trying to wash down the bad taste in his mouth. How he wished old Mrs. Duncan had died of natural causes. It would have made his life so much easier.

Zelma hobbled about in her unhurried manner. She took a can from the pantry and stuck it under an automatic opener. At its gentle whir, the cat appeared, pushing through the swinging door that led in from the dining room.

"Nice kitty, pretty kitty," Biddle said to the copper-hued critter as it swished past his legs. But the pug-nosed feline ignored him entirely.

Zelma drained the can then dumped its contents into a saucer. She turned and hesitated, her Coke-bottle gaze on

Lady Godiva. "Well, here it is," she announced, plunking the dish to the floor with a clatter. "It's tuna fish and no complaining 'cause that's all there is for now."

Biddle half expected the cat to respond.

Instead, Lady Godiva picked her way across the floor to sniff at the offering. Then she lifted her flat face to Zelma and let out an unfriendly hiss. With a flick of her tail, she left as she'd come.

Biddle chuckled. "She's a finicky one."

"She'll be back, believe me," Zelma told him, hands on ill-defined hips. "Miss Nora spoiled her rotten, buying her gourmet cat food like she was royalty." The wrinkled face fell further. "But the men last night took all the fancy slop when they emptied the fridge, and I don't aim to drive all the way back to Alton to get any more, not when I'm in the state I am. There's plenty of tuna besides."

Biddle knew the price of a can of StarKist, and he figured that if tuna was coming down in the world, the cat was doing pretty well.

Zelma wiped off her hands before taking a seat across the table. "So," she said and fixed her eyes on him, "you wanted to ask me some questions about Miss Nora?"

"If you wouldn't mind," he murmured. The old girl did look rather pale.

"I'll do anything to help, Sheriff." Zelma stared down at her hands. "Miss Nora meant more to me than you'll ever know."

"You were close?"

"As close as they come." Zelma let out a tearful sniff. "I've worked here for most of my life. I was here when she and Mr. Duncan first married and when Jim came along. I could never imagine leaving."

Biddle waited for the waterfall, but Zelma brushed at her cheeks and went on.

"She was like family, Sheriff. 'What would we do without each other, Zelma?' she always said." The faded eyes clouded. "But now I'll have to do without her, won't I? She's gone forever. She's not coming back." Zelma sobbed and reached her hand across the table. "What'll I do without her?" she whispered. "What'll I do?"

The sheriff stared at the outstretched fingers, thick at the knuckles and as wrinkled as the rest of her. He wondered what there was for him to say. How was he supposed to comfort the grieving? Sometimes words only seemed to make things worse.

"I'm sorry, ma'am," he got out.

Zelma sighed and withdrew her hand, setting it down in her lap.

Frank shifted in his seat. "Um, ma'am, could you tell me more about yesterday afternoon? Was Mrs. Duncan the only one who was here?"

"Oh, no," the housekeeper said, "hardly the only one. She was trying to nap, and they all showed up one after the other. Miss Nora was quite irritated."

Frank leaned forward. "So who else dropped in?"

Zelma fiddled with her lace collar. "Miss Nora figured so many came because of her nearly being run down. She felt like they'd stopped by to see if she'd really escaped harm. They hoped she was on her deathbed, or that's how Miss Nora saw it. She as good as called them vultures."

"Is that so?" Frank pulled his pad of paper from his pocket, dislodged the pencil, and flipped to a blank page. "Can you recall their names?" he asked. "And perhaps the times they came?"

"Oh, goodness, let me think." Zelma looked suddenly befuddled. "Let's see, I got back from Alton after lunch, and Miss Nora, she was fighting mad at me. She claimed I'd left the front door wide open and the cat had gotten out."

"The names of her visitors, ma'am," the sheriff prodded.

"Well, there was Miss Jean, of course, bringing that food with her. She was the first of them," Zelma said, counting on her fingers. "Then I think Miss Jemima was next."

"Jemima Winthrop?" Frank asked.

Zelma nodded. "She said she wanted to talk to Miss Nora about land. She had plans to build a new library."

"A new library? Hmm." The sheriff hadn't realized they needed one. River Bend already had a perfectly good library as it was.

"Miss Nora didn't like the idea either," Zelma told him. "But Miss Winthrop kept at Miss Nora, demanding back five acres near the harbor that used to belong to her family. She'd been trying to get Miss Nora to deed the land to her. Miss Winthrop wanted to put up a bigger library and name it after her father." The housekeeper shook her head and sighed. "Miss Nora didn't want any part of it, and Miss Jemima didn't like that much."

Frank jotted down more notes. He was certainly aware

of the friction between the Winthrops and the Duncans. It was as much a part of the town's folklore as the red-roofed lighthouse near the river, which residents swore up and down had guided Samuel Clemens safely through a storm during his days as a riverboat pilot.

"Did you ever leave Miss Winthrop alone in the kitchen?" Frank asked.

Zelma paused. "Well, I guess I did. She waited while I went off to tell Miss Nora she'd come. Only I was ordered to send her packing as well."

"I see." Biddle scribbled again.

"And then Mr. Baskin came by"—Zelma stopped and cocked her head—"or was it Mr. Duncan? Both of them asked to see Miss Nora. Well, Mr. Duncan demanded it."

Biddle glanced up. "You didn't happen to leave each of them alone in the kitchen, too?"

"What else could I do?" Zelma looked hurt. "I couldn't just spring them on Miss Nora without warning her first. She would've had my head."

"I understand, Miss Burdine," Biddle told her, sure that facing her angry mistress would have been worse than turning away unwanted guests. "I'm sure you did everything just as you were told."

Zelma smiled sadly. "I did my best, that's true, and it was hard enough, let me tell you. Keeping things ship-shape around here isn't easy. The house is as big as a fortress. You ever dust fourteen rooms, Sheriff, or vacuum fourteen rugs?" Her shoulders stooped as if they bore the weight of the world.

"No, I can't say that I have," he admitted. "I think it's amazing you've done it all on your own."

Zelma's eyes seemed to soften. Or else it was just those damned glasses distorting them.

Frank cleared his throat. "Let's get back to Floyd Baskin. Can you give me an idea what he was after?"

"Why, he wanted money, of course, for his cause," Zelma said matter-of-factly.

The sheriff knew Baskin and his cause very well indeed. "So he came by to get a donation for Save the River?"

"A donation?" Zelma repeated and laughed. "When he was alive, Mr. Duncan practically supported Baskin's efforts single-handedly. When he died, he left them some kind of annual stipend. Only Miss Nora didn't like the turn they'd taken." Zelma let out a noisy *tsk-tsk*. "All they seemed to do lately was break into buildings, destroy property, and the like. Miss Nora had her lawyers working on a loophole to stop the payments."

Frank's heart beat a little bit faster. "You said Mr. Duncan was here as well."

"Yes, the younger brother, Stanley," Zelma offered.

The sheriff detected a hint of pink in her cheeks—even a flash of fear in her eyes—at the mention of Stanley's name.

Zelma folded her hands on the table, and he saw they were trembling. "Miss Nora turned him away, too. Only he came again this morning," she said, and her voice shook. "He tore up the place looking for money."

Frank stopped writing. "So there was bad blood between him and Eleanora?"

Zelma nodded. "The younger Mr. Duncan was the black

sheep of the family, Miss Nora called him. Mr. Marvin, now there was a fine man. Worked hard all his life for every penny he earned. But Mr. Stanley didn't like to sweat. He depended on his brother for everything." Zelma grimaced. "When the younger Mr. Duncan ran through what Mr. Marvin had left him, Miss Nora paid him off, just to keep him away. But yesterday when he showed up, she told me she was finished with him. She was cutting him off cold."

Zelma sniffled. "But he did come back, and if it wasn't for Mrs. Evans showing up when she did, he would have torn up the whole house and not just the library." The woman's owlish eyes fixed on him again, looking petrified. "He said he'll be back, Sheriff, that he won't let me rest until he gets what he wants."

The sheriff hardly heard the last part of it. His ears had ceased listening when he'd heard the words "Mrs. Evans."

He cleared his throat. "Mrs. Evans was here earlier?"

Zelma nodded.

Frank pursed his lips. Didn't that woman ever stay home?

"And thank God for her, too," the housekeeper told him. "She chased him off. Threatened to call you up and turn him in."

"Right," Frank said dryly.

"Is there anything else, Sheriff?" Zelma was biting at her lip as if she might burst into tears.

"Just one more thing, ma'am, and then I'll go," he said. "Did Miss Nora ask you where the goose liver had come from?"

"No." Zelma sounded repentant. "She wouldn't have

eaten a bite if she'd realized Miss Jean had brought it over, so I didn't say a word. I didn't figure there was any harm in it. Despite what Miss Nora believed, I rather liked Miss Jean. I didn't blame her for what happened to Jim." Her teeth gnawed her bottom lip. "If I'd have mentioned where it came from, Miss Nora never would've eaten any of it. She would have made me throw it all away. Oh, dear!"

Zelma sobbed, and Biddle glanced up at her from his notepad. "Are you okay, ma'am?"

"Please, Sheriff, I'm not feeling so good all of a sudden." The woman pushed up her glasses to dab at her eyes with her apron. "It's just that I'm so tired. I didn't sleep well last night. I'm not used to being alone, and poor Lady howled until morning."

He tucked the pencil and pad into his shirt pocket. "You've been real helpful, ma'am. If you don't mind, though, I'd like to take another look around."

Zelma struggled to her feet. "Might I go lay down? I'm feeling dizzy."

Frank nodded. "Please don't worry about me. I can let myself out when I'm done."

The old girl disappeared as fast as she could shuffle out, and Frank didn't waste a single second. He pulled on a pair of disposable gloves before opening up the cabinets under the sink. That was where his Sarah kept everything, from dishwashing liquid to carpet cleaner to pot scrubbers and insecticides.

He found a trash bag from a box set against the drainpipe then dropped in a few cans and bottles of poisons aimed at killing any kind of bug infestation.

Frank hated to admit it, but maybe Helen Evans wasn't so off base after all. Maybe there was more to this case than the obvious.

If the food Jean had left for Eleanora had been in the refrigerator all of yesterday afternoon, it meant any of Eleanora's drop-in visitors could have had access to the goose liver, not to mention the motive and means to murder old Mrs. Duncan. And it would only have taken a matter of minutes.

Chapter 12

HELEN WALKED AWAY from Jean's house and headed up Bluff Street toward a grassy spot with a wrought-iron bench. She sat down and took in the view of the river. The water sparkled so brilliantly beneath the sun that it almost fooled her into thinking it was blue and not a muddy brown.

But her mind wasn't on the Mississippi or the lovely view.

Instead she thought of Jean and how she'd reacted to Biddle's visit. At first she'd seemed as genuinely taken aback as Helen had been by the sheriff's announcement that Eleanora had been poisoned. But Jean had recovered awfully quickly. Her voice sounding distant, she'd been cool as a cucumber as she'd answered Biddle's questions. It had reminded Helen of a student reciting a memorized lesson. When Helen had sought Jean out after Frank Biddle had left, she'd found her calmly thumbing through a cookbook in the kitchen.

"Are you all right?" Helen had asked.

Jean had glanced up, worry creasing her forehead. "You won't tell anyone about this, will you, Helen? If word gets out that I'm under suspicion for poisoning Eleanora with my pâté, I'll never get another job in this town or anywhere else. The LCIL will probably drop me from catering the luncheon, and I don't even want to think about losing that job in St. Louis."

Wow, Helen remembered thinking.

She felt the same now. It was like stumbling into an old episode of *Twilight Zone*.

Maybe Jean was going through some sort of denial. The woman had lost her husband tragically just two years before. Then her mother-in-law had blamed her for Jim's death. It had taken an enormous amount of willpower for Jean to pick herself up and move on. Now Eleanora was dead, and it was Jean's goose liver that had killed her.

Helen could hardly fault her friend for her strange behavior. Perhaps Jean didn't have the strength to deal with another death, not so soon and not this way.

Helen sighed, praying this would all be over with posthaste. Jean needed to get on with her life and her brand-new catering business. How could she do either with the suspicion of murder hanging over her head?

Helen shifted uncomfortably on the wrought iron bench.

Frank Biddle would find the perpetrator, wouldn't he? He wouldn't try to pin this on Jean? Sometimes it seemed to Helen that River Bend's sheriff tended to focus only on the obvious rather than looking any deeper.

She felt her chest constrict.

What if he'd gotten it into his head already that Jean did it, no matter who else had a reason? And Helen knew there were plenty who did. Eleanora hadn't reached eighty years old and accumulated such wealth without making a few enemies along the way.

Would Biddle do a thorough investigation, looking beyond Jean for suspects?

Helen had to believe that he would. He might be stubborn, but he was a good man and he wanted to do the right thing. He reminded Helen of her late husband in some respects: stubborn, unbendable, and unwilling to look to the left or right when he was sure the answer lay smack down the middle.

Don't let yourself get dragged into this one, she could hear Biddle saying, *it's not your concern.*

Helen frowned, feeling rankled by his warning.

Let it go?

Ha.

Telling Helen to stop protecting her friend was a lot like asking Amber to stop chasing mice or rabbits or birds. It wasn't going to happen.

With that settled—in her own mind anyhow—she got up from the bench and dusted off her pants. Then she meandered down Harbor Drive.

When she reached the turnoff that would take her toward Main Street, she paused to lift a hand above her eyes, squinting at what looked like half a dozen people marching up and down the docks with signs. Others stood nearby in a cluster, simply watching.

What in the world was going on?

Helen's curiosity got the better of her, and she by-passed the sidewalk, cutting across the grass toward the harbor. The nearer she got, the louder the voices became. They chanted, "Stop the killing, save the river . . . stop the killing, save the river," shaking their signs all the while.

As she approached the docks, the fishy odor of the water filled her nose, and Helen caught herself holding her breath. She headed over to the clump of spectators, who murmured among each other and stared at the goings-on with wide eyes. She noticed then that several men with fishing gear were attempting to descend the steps to the docks, but the sign-wielding protestors blocked their path. Between the curses and the chanting, Helen could hardly hear herself think.

She spotted her bridge partner, Clara Foley, among the onlookers. Dressed in a hot pink muumuu, she would have been hard to miss. Helen shouted her name and Clara waved, her dimpled face beaming beneath her graying Gibson girl bun.

"What's this about?" Helen asked when she reached her side.

"It's that Floyd Baskin and his loony tunes," Clara told her loudly enough to make herself heard above the racket. "They won't let anyone onto their boats."

"Has someone called the sheriff?"

Clara's eyes twinkled, as if she was enjoying every minute. "I understand he's on his way."

Helen turned her gaze to the protestors, easily picking

out Floyd Baskin from the pack. His bearded face looked the same as it had on television weeks ago when he'd been tossed in jail for his stunt at the utility plant: flushed, fiery, and determined. He wore jeans and a plaid flannel shirt with the sleeves rolled up, his figure lean and wiry. He probably kept in shape, she figured, by marching around all day and pumping signs.

Helen squinted at the one he held now, which proclaimed in bold black letters, *Poisoned Water, Poisoned Fish!* Another sign drawn in crimson screamed, *Stop Murdering the Mississippi!* And a third declared, *The Blood's on Your Hands!*

"Oh, dear," she murmured, wondering what they thought they'd accomplish by picketing on the docks when all they seemed to be doing was antagonizing the fishermen.

The gaggle of men clutching poles and tackle boxes congregated at the top of the wooden stairs, and not one looked even vaguely amused.

They mostly seemed to be trading words with Baskin, though Helen couldn't make out much, as Baskin's comrades chanted every bit as loudly.

A sturdy fellow in a lure-covered hat started to shoulder his way down the steps, only to have Baskin stand right in front of him. As the docks were hardly wider than a yardstick, it didn't leave the fisherman any room to maneuver around him. So after shaking his fist and cursing out Baskin, he, too, backed down.

Did Mr. Baskin imagine this little exhibition was going to win him any supporters? Did he actually think it might cause more of the townsfolk to write him checks and eagerly send him donations?

Helen would have bet that most of the fisherman had sympathized with Baskin's cause before. But trying to keep the sportsmen from their boats only made them angry. Hardly the way to shore up your supporters, she mused.

"He's coming!" the spectators murmured, and Helen felt Clara's elbow nudge her side.

She looked toward the graveled parking lot to see Biddle's squad car pulling up. He emerged seconds after. His hands balled into fists as he approached, and his hound dog's face appeared as grim as it had been this morning when he'd appeared on Jean's doorstep.

Helen peered at him over Clara's shoulder.

"All right. Enough," he said, sounding beyond fed up. "The show's over, so why doesn't everyone just go on home?"

No one budged.

"Okay, fine, stay right where you are," he told them. "But keep back from the docks. We don't want anyone falling in."

"Or you might turn into a two-headed turtle," Clara murmured.

Helen glanced toward the harbor water, shuddering at the thought of toppling into the smelly, opaque brown. She could only imagine what kinds of bacteria and sludge lay beneath the surface.

The sheriff pushed up his hat and scratched at his near-bald head as though contemplating his course of action.

Then he tugged his hat back down and stomped toward the docks, heading for the group of fishermen.

Helen watched as Frank Biddle hooked his thumbs in his gun belt, apparently listening while the fishermen did a lot of pointing and yelling.

The sheriff made his way around the men and their gear until he stood nose to nose with Baskin.

"We're not leaving until we get everyone in town to listen," Baskin hollered, his voice megaphone loud. "Don't you get it? The river is poisoned. Every citizen of River Bend would stand behind us if they were made to drink this very water and breathe it, like the fish!"

"We just want to get to our boats," the fisherman nearest Frank Biddle yelled. "So take your nutty pals and shove off."

"Over my dead body!" Baskin fired back.

"Hey, now, let's take this down a notch," the sheriff said and patted the air with a palm. "Mr. Baskin, I don't believe you filed for a permit to picket. So you need to get your folks and head out, or else I'll have to—"

"Arrest us?" Baskin said, interrupting. "What are you going to do, put us all in handcuffs and throw us in a holding cell?"

"If I have to," the sheriff told him.

"Then do it!" Baskin replied, and his contingent lined up right behind him. "But you'll have to drag us off, because we're not going willingly."

"I'll drag you off, you loudmouthed son of a—"

Helen flinched as one of the fishermen got around the sheriff and charged Baskin, knocking him off the dock and sending them both splashing down into the murky water. Before Helen could see either emerge, Baskin's sign popped up and floated across the frothy brown surface.

Then another fisherman bypassed Biddle and swung at the nearest protestor, the pair plunging into the harbor next.

"Oh, dear," Helen murmured, shaking her head.

Though Clara Foley seemed far more amused. She had to slap a hand across her mouth to mask her laughter.

The sheriff seemed to be doing his best to stay out of the path of the fishermen, who wheedled their way around him and tackled the remaining protestors until not one was left standing. Muddy water splashed onto the docks, soaking the wood as the fight continued in the harbor.

Helen knew the harbor wasn't deep, and she imagined the viscous mud at the bottom sucking shoes off feet. She only hoped there weren't any water moccasins in the vicinity. The last thing Sheriff Biddle needed was to have to deal with a bunch of very angry, waterlogged, and snake-bitten men.

A young girl standing with her mother jostled Helen as the child dug into her pockets to retrieve a pink plastic whistle. Almost timidly at first she gave it a few quick toots. Urged on by the crowd, she put out several shrill bursts that made Helen's ears ring for a few minutes afterward.

But the splashing and the fighting abruptly stopped.

Once Frank Biddle stopped wincing, he gave a jerk of his thumb as he shouted, "I hope that cooled you off. Everyone out of the water! And I mean right now! Pick up your signs and go home, you hear?" As Floyd Baskin flung a leg over the dock and dragged himself up, the sheriff put a hand on his soggy shoulder. "Not you, Mr. Baskin. I want a word with you in my office. I've got a tarp in the trunk you can sit on so you don't foul up my car."

Grumbling about missing a day's catch, the soggy fishermen squished off with their rods and tackle boxes and cartons of fresh bait. The equally soaked protestors straggled off in the opposite direction.

Helen watched as Biddle nudged Baskin away from the docks toward the squad car. They came close enough that the bearded Baskin had a chance to pause and glare at the lingering onlookers; close enough for Helen to get a whiff of the man as well. It was enough to make her nose wrinkle.

Without warning, Baskin spat in the grass in front of Clara Foley. Helen wasn't the only one who jumped back a step.

"Poison," he said, the fire in his eyes not dampened by the harbor waters that dripped from his hair and beard and clothes. "How'd you like to take a drink of that, huh? How'd you like to swallow something so toxic?"

Clara made a noise of disgust and huddled behind Helen.

Frank Biddle's gaze met Helen's for an instant before he grabbed hold of Baskin's wet shirt and dragged the man away.

"What a dreadful person," the mother of the girl with the whistle murmured.

"Can you believe his tactics?" another remarked.

"I hope Biddle locks him up this time!"

Voices rattled on behind her, but Helen shut them out. All she could hear were Baskin's shouts about swallowing poison. She kept her eyes on the squad car as it pulled away from the graveled lot in a cloud of dust. Despite the warmth of the afternoon sun, she shivered.

Chapter 13

FRANK BIDDLE LEANED his forearms on his desk, taking in the sight of Floyd Baskin.

No one ever looked entirely comfortable seated in the chair across from him, for obvious reasons. But Baskin appeared as out of place as anyone he'd ever seen.

The fellow didn't sit so much as slump, his long legs stretched out before him, his tennis shoes caked with mud. With his head leaned back against the wood slats, his eyes watched Biddle in return, the only sign that he was anxious in the least besides the curl of his fingertips around the armrests.

Water had settled into small puddles beneath him. A trail of wet footprints led from the door. Biddle thought of his squad car, and he sighed. He'd tried to get the man to sit on a tarp, but he'd refused. So the black-and-white's backseat and floor mats were equally begrimed.

He scratched his thumb against his jaw, figuring he'd

have to take a towel to it all when he'd finished up here. Baskin himself could use a good soaping, what with the way he smelled: like the river during drought season, when the water was low and fish washed up on the rocky banks like shells on the shoreline.

Frank cleared his throat and shifted in his chair, Baskin's unblinking gaze getting to him, as he was sure it was meant to. He steepled his fingers under his chin and remarked, "I heard you were at Eleanora Duncan's yesterday afternoon."

Baskin's head lifted. He squinted. "What?"

Doubtless he'd assumed Biddle had brought him in to give him a lecture about picketing on the docks.

Well, he was dead wrong.

"I said I heard you were over at old Mrs. Duncan's yesterday. You want to fill me in on why you were there?"

Baskin pulled himself up a little straighter, sitting stiff-backed in the chair. An improvement in posture, perhaps, but he didn't look any friendlier for it. "Why do you care where I was? And don't say it's because Queen Eleanora complained. Hell, I never even saw her. She had that dim-witted maid of hers send me away." Something flickered in the dark of his eyes. "Besides, I know she's dead. She had a heart attack or something. Word's all over town." He smiled thinly. "And no one can file charges from the grave, can they, Sheriff?"

"She didn't die of a heart attack," Frank told him, and though Baskin's smile wavered, it remained on his face, peeking out from his beard. "Or of any other natural causes."

"What'd she do?" the man asked, not sounding sympathetic in the least. "Overdose on prune juice? Take too many Maalox?"

"She was poisoned."

Baskin's grin vanished. He drew his legs up, leaving a trail of mud where his sneakers slid across the wood.

"You act surprised."

The spark returned to Baskin's gaze. "Of course I'm surprised." His forehead wrinkled deeply, sending the slashes of gray brows lower over his eyes. "You're not insinuating that I had something to do with it?"

"Did you?"

Baskin leaned back in the chair again, his long legs stuck out. His "hell if I'm gonna let you get to me" position, Frank figured. Baskin had had plenty of practice at it, and it showed.

Frank picked up a pencil and tapped it against the palm of his hand. "Seems to me you're awfully fired up about poisoning. Didn't you tell those folks when I was dragging you off that they'd change their tune fast enough if they were to swallow something toxic?"

"If you'd paid attention, you'd know what I meant," Baskin snapped. "I was talking about the poisoning of the river, mucking up the water with sewage and plant waste and killing everything living in it with chemicals. *That* kind of poison." He spat out the words as if even they tasted rank.

Frank rolled the pencil between his fingers, never taking his eyes off Baskin. He liked to watch the play of emotions on his face, the quick shift of his gaze. "You still haven't answered my question about why you tried to see Eleanora Duncan. What would she want with someone like you?"

"I was there for humanitarian reasons, if you will," Baskin said, though the line sounded more like a rehearsed phrase than an honest response. "I'd heard she'd nearly gotten run over in the street, and I thought I'd check up on her. You know, see how she was holding up." His fingers loosened on the armrest then tightened again. "She was a big contributor to Save the River. Well, her husband was anyway. He was a fine man, even remembered us in his will. The money we've received from the estate these past two years since he died, it's what's kept us running if you must know the truth."

Frank recalled what Zelma Burdine had told him earlier about Eleanora's lawyers looking for a loophole in Marvin's will to stop further payments to Baskin. Funny Baskin hadn't mentioned that.

"You're wondering why Mr. Duncan helped us out in particular, aren't you, Sheriff? Him being such a well-respected businessman in these parts," Baskin rattled on, leaning forward in the chair, elbows on his knees. "He could've donated to any cause, isn't that what you're thinking?"

"It crossed my mind," Frank muttered and tried to keep his expression stoic. Sarah was always saying he had a face as telling as a billboard.

"We fund research as well," Baskin explained, and his bearded face appeared less sullen and more animated. "We're trying to find ways to clean the water without causing further damage to the environment. And we're studying a legal means of increasing EPA pressure on the plants that dump waste unchecked." Then the fight returned to his eyes. He came out of his chair for a moment, his hands gesturing. "We *have* to make a lot of noise, don't you see? That's the only way we get heard. If we sat on our butts making phone calls and acting like a bunch of church ladies, no one would pay us the slightest attention. You think the press is gonna cover anything I do if I act like Pollyanna?"

Frank didn't respond. He couldn't think of what to say, except that Baskin was probably right. A Goody Two-shoes wouldn't make headlines these days. Nope, the only stories that the TV, print papers, and Internet news seemed to want to cover concerned serial killers, terrorists, and lunatics like Baskin.

"The old woman didn't understand what we were about. She had no idea what we were doing and its importance." Baskin's voice rose and his skin flushed. He cut himself off, his face closing up like a door slamming shut.

"Go on," Frank urged, waiting to see if Baskin would admit that Eleanora had been trying hard to cut off Save the River permanently.

"Like I said, she just didn't sympathize with our cause, not like her husband had," Baskin finished, offering nothing more.

"I see," the sheriff remarked, and he did see very well indeed. Without Eleanora Duncan around, Floyd Baskin didn't have to worry about his cash cow being slaughtered.

Baskin stared at him, unflinching. "Are you through with me now?"

"That depends." Frank set down his pencil and folded his arms across his chest. "Is there anything else you'd like to say about your visit to Eleanora Duncan's house on the day she died? You didn't go by to threaten her, by chance?"

Baskin's answer was a silent glare.

"All right, then." Obviously Floyd Baskin wasn't going to make this easy for him. "You can go, but don't go far," Frank told him.

Baskin rose from the chair, his soggy clothing clinging to his lean frame. He ran a hand over his damp hair. "Unless you want to arrest me, General, I'm off," he said, and, when Biddle didn't respond, he saluted him, his eyes bright and lips upturned, the mockery in the gesture more than evident.

Frank felt his cheeks burn, but he held himself in check. Part of being a cop was knowing how to handle those without respect for authority. Still, it took everything he had not to slap some cuffs on Baskin and toss him into a cell just to teach him a lesson.

Baskin's sneakers squished noisily as he walked to the door and let himself out, closing it behind him with a slam.

His gaze on the door, the sheriff swallowed, though the lump in his throat seemed inclined to remain. He didn't like that fellow. Didn't like him one bit.

And he didn't trust him any better.

Chapter 14

HELEN WASN'T IN any mood to fix dinner for one.

The day had been long enough as it was, what with the LCIL meeting in the morning, then finding Stanley Duncan tearing up Eleanora's house, not to mention Biddle's dropping in at Jean's to tell them Eleanora had been poisoned and then insinuating that Jean was his prime suspect. And, last but certainly not least, there was that scene at the harbor with Floyd Baskin's troupe duking it out with the local fishermen.

What, she wondered, was happening to this town?

River Bend was usually so quiet. Well, quiet by today's standards. Save for the occasional potlucks and auctions, church meetings, bridge games and bingo, not much went on to surprise its residents from week to week.

Until Frank Biddle had dropped the bomb about Eleanora being murdered.

Helen still couldn't believe it.

If she closed her eyes, she could picture Eleanora's face and the fear in her expression as she'd pulled her out of the way of the speeding car. "I think somebody's trying to kill me," she'd said, words Helen couldn't shake.

If only she'd gotten a better look at that sedan, if only she'd seen who'd been at the wheel. If she'd caught even a part of the license plate, the sheriff would have had something more to go on.

Stop it. Just stop it, she told herself. What good did it do now for her to surmise? It certainly wouldn't bring Eleanora back, and it wouldn't do diddlysquat to help catch the killer.

Helen went into the bathroom and ran the cold water, dampening a washcloth to press to her cheeks and brow. She toweled off after, and her gaze drifted over to the bathtub.

She sighed.

Soaking in lavender-scented bubbles might be just the thing to relax her. The idea of it certainly sounded better than cooking over a hot stove or, rather, in her microwave.

Her stomach grumbled, and she realized she'd better do something to feed herself. Dinner first. Bath second.

She headed into the kitchen, nearly stumbling over Amber, who seemed to dart out of nowhere. Where food was concerned, he had remarkable kitty radar. He sat down near his empty saucer, watching her with eyes as yellow as his name.

Amber mewed, and Helen smiled weakly.

"Okay, okay, I'll get your supper," she gave in. "What'll it be tonight, huh? Cod 'n' Salmon? No? How about Turkey 'n' Giblets?"

So long as it wasn't goose liver, she found herself thinking as she opened the can and plunked the food into a clean dish. The watery sauce that came with it splashed over and onto the countertop, making a smelly mess.

Helen wiped up the slop then set the bowl down for the cat. He sniffed suspiciously before he began to gulp down the contents without bothering to chew.

Still bent over, she spotted a smattering of ants racing about. What with all the goings-on, she'd nearly forgotten about her infestation. She'd meant to put down some Splat, but she'd been interrupted by Jean's phone call.

Well, better late than never, she mused, and brought out the insecticide from under the sink, where she'd stowed it when she'd unpacked the groceries.

She'd bought Splat often enough to know how to use it without bothering with the instructions—which she couldn't read without her glasses anyway, and those, she recalled, were out on the porch beside her unfinished crossword.

Tearing up the tiny piece of cardboard provided in the box, she dampened each square with the liquid before placing them strategically beside the floorboards where the ants seemed to be coming in. She did make sure they were well away from Amber's food. The last thing she wanted was for her old tom to play with poison. Although Amber didn't seem any too concerned about what she was doing. He gobbled up his meal, ignoring her entirely.

When she was done, Helen put away the tiny bottle of Splat and washed her hands. Then she picked up her purse and headed for the diner.

The walk wasn't long, and, with the night settling in on the valley, the evening was a pleasant one. The air felt cool but not too cool, the breeze just enough to tickle her nose with the scent of wild honeysuckle and sweet peas.

She breathed in deeply, listening to the even tread of her steps on the pavement, waving to those who called out greetings from their porches. All she wanted was a hot meal served by Erma. Afterward, she was sliding into the bathtub as quickly as she could draw the water and pour in the bubbles one of her granddaughters had given her last Christmas. She intended to soak until the cows came home or until the water got cold, whichever came first. Then she'd put on her softest nightgown and climb into bed with a good book. Maybe that new culinary murder mystery she'd picked up at the library the day before.

No, she decided, that probably wouldn't help her sleep at all.

Helen quickened her pace, seeing the light from the diner spilling onto the sidewalk about a block ahead in the midst of downtown.

She tucked her purse more tightly into the crook of her elbow, glancing around her as she hustled. She'd definitely make sure the doors were locked tonight, although admittedly she often didn't bother. People watched out for each other in River Bend. Really bad things weren't supposed to happen here like they did in big cities.

But life seemed different these days, and crime had reared its ugly head in this small community too often of late. Now Eleanora was dead, and Helen felt unnerved in a way she hadn't since Joe had died those three years ago and she'd been alone for the first time in her life.

It frightened her to think that whoever had murdered the poor dear might be someone Eleanora had known for years.

Like Jean.

The thought buzzed around and around like a pesky mosquito.

Helen scolded herself.

How could she doubt her friend? Of course Jean wasn't guilty. Helen simply would not believe that Jim Duncan's widow could have actually put some type of poison into Eleanora's pâté to rid herself of a mother-in-law who treated her badly. And if the sheriff couldn't see that Jean didn't have it in her, Helen would have to find a way to convince him. There were plenty of others who disliked Eleanora as much as, if not more than, Jean did.

What about Stanley Duncan? Helen mused. There was clearly no love lost between him and Eleanora. Maybe he'd figured that with the wife of his dead brother out of the picture, he could stake claim to the Duncan fortune. After all, as he'd pointed out, he was the last of the family, what with Jim having been killed in the accident. He was the only blood relative remaining, anyway, as Jean was Jim's wife, or, rather, his widow.

Oh, dear.

Helen frowned, coming to a stop.

It all came back to Jean, didn't it?

She shook away the niggling sense of uncertainty that prickled the hair at the back of her neck, and she looked up to find herself past the diner, nearly past the two blocks of downtown altogether.

Helen gazed at the playground that sat beyond a stone wall and meandering creek. The swings and slides were bathed in darkness and deserted at this hour. Beyond the bridge glowed the white clapboard of the chapel, its steeple poking up into the twilight.

She started to turn around and head back when something caught her eye.

Someone was emerging from the wooden playhouse behind the swings. Helen couldn't tell much about the shadowy shape until the figure crossed the bridge over the creek and passed beneath the streetlamp.

Jemima Winthrop?

Helen nearly called out to her, but Jemima quickly scurried off in the opposite direction.

Whatever had the woman been doing at the playground, of all places, particularly in the dark and all alone?

Or perhaps she wasn't alone.

Another shadowy figure ducked out of the playhouse and crossed the bridge as Jemima had only moments before, pausing briefly beneath the streetlamp before heading up the sidewalk toward Helen.

Uh-oh.

Helen scrambled around the nearest tree and pressed her back to the bark, holding her breath until the footsteps clicked past on the sidewalk. Helen's heartbeat eased only when the sound of them disappeared altogether.

She came out of her hiding place, clutching her purse to her belly, staring up Main Street and wondering what in the world Jemima Winthrop was up to. Because Helen had a feeling she was up to something. Why else would she be meeting with Stanley Duncan at the playground?

It certainly wasn't to discuss his volunteering at the library.

She sighed and headed back to the sidewalk, backtracking to the diner, thinking that Sheriff Biddle certainly had his work cut out for him. The list of those with cause to want Eleanora dead seemed only to grow, not shrink.

Chapter 15

SETTLED INTO A booth at the diner, Helen munched on a salad as she waited for Erma to bring her a bowl of piping hot chili.

Voices hummed around her, and the noise was comforting, familiar. She sat alone, despite an offer from Hilary Dell to join her and Clara Foley at their table.

She looked over at them now and found their eyes on her as well. Clara blushed and turned away. Hilary merely smiled a dimpled grin, primping at her near beehive of silver hair before wiggling her manicured fingers Helen's way.

Helen nodded and went back to eating her salad, plucking out a slice of farm-grown tomato and chewing without tasting. She knew what they were talking about, what everyone else in town was discussing, which was one of the reasons she'd turned down Hilary's invitation.

She wasn't up to gossiping tonight. She didn't want to

natter on about Eleanora's death as if it was simply the latest news flash, no weightier than who'd shown up at church with their slip hanging out or who was having an affair or divorcing or checking into Shady Acres.

She didn't care to hear Hilary's opinion about who did it or Clara's guess as to the culprit, as if it was all just a game.

"Here's your chili, hon." Erma's voice broke through her thoughts, and Helen gazed up past splattered apron and checkerboard pink, into the simple face framed by netted hair. "Hot out of the pot," Erma proclaimed and set down the crockery before picking up the remains of Helen's salad just as quick. "Enjoy."

"I'm sure I will. Thanks."

She hadn't even swallowed the first spoonful of chili when the bell above the door jangled and Fanny Melville bustled in. "Hey, there, Erma dear, I'm here for my order to go."

"Be a minute, hon," the waitress replied from behind the counter, where she refilled coffee cups, cleared plates, and slapped down steaming platters snatched from the kitchen pass-through as if she had more hands than two.

Helen caught Fanny's gaze and her friend sauntered over, setting down her purse on the table. "You know I've been trying to phone you all day," she said grumpily, peering at Helen above the spectacles perched on her nose. She lowered her voice and leaned in. "Amos got back the toxicology report on Eleanora Duncan, and it appears she was—"

"Poisoned, yes, I know," Helen cut in. She hooked a thumb discreetly at Hilary and Clara. "I think everyone in River Bend has heard by now."

Fanny frowned. "Well, I'm sorry, dear, but I did try to tell you first. I phoned you just as soon as I learned."

"I'm sure you did."

"You were out, I guess."

Helen sighed and set down her spoon. "I was," she said, "all day, as a matter of fact."

"So you don't know about Floyd Baskin?"

"You mean the protest? Believe it or not, I was there," Helen admitted.

Fanny laughed. "Oh, I believe it."

"I'm beginning to wonder if it's safe to leave the house."

"Then you probably also know that the sheriff questioned the old hippy." Doc's wife bent forward. "I think he's a suspect."

"Floyd Baskin?" Helen wrinkled her brow. "Why?"

"Why else?" Fanny said, adding, in a whisper, "money."

"Did the sheriff learn anything?"

Fanny shrugged and slipped her purse back over her shoulder. "That I don't know. Though I do have some news I don't think has made its way around town yet. Amos says they're pretty sure they've found the insecticide that killed Eleanora."

Helen sat up straighter.

"The county crime lab is still running more tests, Amos said, and they should know by tomorrow if they've got a match."

"I see."

"Mrs. Melville!" Erma's voice boomed from across the diner. "Your to-go order's ready, hon."

Fanny tapped the table. "Looks like I'm being paged. Bridge still on for tomorrow night? We've already postponed it from tonight, since we had to find a sub for Sarah Biddle."

"Oh, dear, I hadn't even thought about it." Helen wondered if she should cancel altogether. Not that the group had ever let her cancel before, and they probably wouldn't see the need now either. After all, it wasn't any of the regulars who'd been murdered, so they wouldn't need to find another substitute at the last minute. "I guess it's still on," Helen said.

"All right, I'll see you then," Fanny replied with a nod before weaving through the tables to pick up her bagged food at the counter. She paused to gab with Hilary and Clara for a minute before setting the bells to jangling as she departed.

Helen stared after her, wondering who the evidence would point to once all the pieces to the puzzle fell into place.

HELEN SLEPT BADLY that night, plagued by nightmares like she hadn't had since she was a little girl. She awoke in a panic, a heavy weight on her chest, crushing her lungs, only to find Amber slumped across her rib cage, having no trouble snoozing himself. With a grunt, she unceremoniously dumped the old tom onto the bed beside her. He didn't even stir. Then she dragged herself into the bathroom to brush her teeth and comb her hair.

She hadn't taken a bubble bath the night before, so she filled the tub, dumping in plenty of lavender gel. When things were good and frothy, she got in, reclining in the scented water until it cooled and her skin was as wrinkled as Grandma Moses's. Her legs had been achy from all the walking she'd done, but soaking in the bath helped more than a buffered aspirin.

Once she was dressed in her favorite green sweat suit, she felt somewhat better.

Her mood improved even more when she went into the kitchen to find the trail of ants was broken. Only a few bugs still crawled across the linoleum—or, rather, they staggered. More lay dead near the piece of cardboard dabbed with Splat.

A thin smile crossed her lips. She was pleased to see the Splat had worked its magic yet again. If only Sheriff Biddle could be as successful at catching Eleanora's killer.

She fixed herself a bowl of cereal and took it with her out onto the porch. The paperboy was just passing by in his van, gravel popping beneath the tires as he sped through town, tossing copies of the *Alton Telegraph* out the window without even slowing.

Helen heard hers hit the porch steps with a slap. Instinctively, she grabbed the handle of the screen door to pull it open, but it didn't budge. Ah, yes, she'd locked it last night, something she'd rarely done in fifty years in River Bend. She unhooked the latch before retrieving the paper from the stoop.

She picked up her glasses from the sofa before spreading the *Telegraph* on the table before her, eating as she read the morning's headlines.

There it was at the bottom of page one.

WEALTHY RIVER BEND WIDOW MURDERED

A story ran beneath it.

Eleanora Duncan, 80, widow of Marvin Duncan, Duncan Industries, was found dead in her River Bend, IL, home on Monday evening. Dr. Edward Drake, Jersey County Medical Examiner, confirms that autopsy results on Mrs. Duncan have revealed she ingested a poison known as sodium tetraborate often used in over-the-counter insecticides. Sheriff Frank Biddle of River Bend, IL, states that suspects are being questioned, though no arrests have been made at this time.

Oh, dear.

Helen set the paper aside, unable to read another word. She pushed away her cereal bowl, no longer hungry.

It seemed somehow more horrible and all the more real to see it written up in black and white with Eleanora's picture staring out from amidst the page. Helen found herself suddenly tempted to crawl back into bed and hide under the covers until all was well.

Whenever that may be, she mused with a sigh.

If there was only some way she could help, some way

she could find the answers that pointed to who did it. But what did she know that Frank Biddle hadn't probably found out already? All she had were her eyes and ears, and even they weren't as sharp as they used to be.

"Helen? Yoo hoo, are you there?" someone called from the road. Moments after, there came the thump of feet up the front steps.

Helen took off her glasses and squinted at the hazy figure on the other side of the screen. "Clara?" she said.

"Mind if I come in?"

Helen didn't even have a chance to answer.

Clara Foley pushed the screen door open so fast the spring squealed. With a slap, it dropped shut behind her.

The sight of the bright orange muumuu hit Helen's eyes like the sun on chrome, and she felt the need to put up a hand to shield them.

"I was just down at the diner for some bacon and eggs, and I saw your friend Jean," Clara started in with such a flush to her cheeks that Helen knew there was more coming.

She only hoped none of the gossips had linked Jean to the poison. So far as Helen was aware, no one in River Bend beyond herself, Jean, and the sheriff knew it was Jean's pâté that had been spiked with sodium tetraborate.

"You saw Jean," she prodded, trying to keep the worry from her voice.

Clara pulled out a wicker chair and plunked herself down at the table, waving a hand toward the Alton newspaper. "Been reading about the murder, I see."

"Hard to avoid, isn't it? It's more like sensationalism

than hard news the way they make everything seem so scandalous these days."

Clara chuckled, her shoulders shaking. Wisps of gray escaped from the poof of her bun, though Clara brushed them from her brow with a fast sweep of her fingers. "Everyone's talking about it, of course. You should've heard the crowd at the diner."

"I can well imagine," Helen murmured, figuring no topic in this town was sacrosanct.

"Anyway," Clara said and took in a deep breath, making Helen wonder if she hadn't run all the way over. "I'd just finished the last of my toast when I looked out the window and saw the sheriff's car pulling in across the way."

Helen sat up straighter.

"He had someone with him, you see." Her pale eyes widened, and her voice rattled with excitement. "It was Jean Duncan, as it turns out. He hustled her into his office pretty quick-like, which made me wonder if he didn't haul her down there on official business, seeing as how it's so early in the morning and the expression on his face wasn't any too friendly." Clara paused for breath before rushing on. "And Jean, well, she looked like he'd dragged her out of bed and she'd thrown on the first thing she could find. Her blouse was hanging out of her blue jeans, and her hair looked positively wild. . . . "

Helen was out of her seat and to the door before Clara had finished.

She heard her friend calling her back, but she didn't even turn around.

Moving as fast as her legs would carry her, Helen followed the sidewalk away from the intersection of Jersey and Springfield, heading for downtown.

By the time she reached the sheriff's office, she was out of breath, so that she had to stop outside the door, put her hands on her knees, and gulp at the air, trying to get her wind back. Even then, she could hear the voices from inside.

There was Frank Biddle's familiar monotone, which—when she had her sense of humor intact—she thought sounded like a pretty good imitation of James Arness's Marshal Dillon. And there was Jean's voice, sounding so high-pitched that Helen knew she was near to tears.

Helen didn't hesitate another minute.

She wiped her hands on her pants, grabbed the door handle, and pushed her way in, leaving the bright of early morning for the dim of inside.

The voices hushed at the slam of the door.

Helen held her chin high as she strode past the bulletin board crammed with notices for garage sales and free pups, as well as MOST WANTED posters with penciled-out teeth and drawn-on mustaches.

"Mrs. Evans, what in blazes are you doing here?" Biddle sputtered, half rising behind his paper-cluttered desk.

She ignored him and approached the chair in which Jean sat. Her friend looked up at her, the worry plain on her face, her eyes moist, her skin bare of makeup. Her silver hair, usually so neatly coiffed in a scarf-tied ponytail, appeared disheveled. Her blouse looked rumpled and it was, as Clara had mentioned, hanging loose at the hem. For heaven's sake, were those slippers on her feet?

That alone got Helen's dander up.

She put her hands on Jean's shoulders and stared straight at Biddle. "What's going on here?" she asked in a tone that had once sparked fear in the hearts of her own children. "Is this how you're operating now, Sheriff, shaking women out of bed and dragging them off like hardened criminals?"

Biddle didn't appear any too pleased by her accusation. From his neck to his near-bald crown, he flushed an improbable purple. "You need to stay out of this, ma'am," he said and shook a finger at her. "This is none of your business. You're meddling in a murder investigation."

Helen blinked. "I'm what?"

"You heard me," he told her, frowning. "And I'd appreciate it very much if you'd just go on home."

"I will not!" Helen stood her ground, tightening her hold on Jean, who lifted a hand to cover hers. "I'm not moving an inch until you tell me why you've brought Jean here," she said and somehow managed to sound less strident. "I don't mean to interfere with your work, Sheriff, truly I don't," she added, trying her best to pacify him, knowing that to do otherwise might hurt Jean, not help her. "But I simply can't mind my own business when a friend is in trouble."

Biddle looked mighty huffy, but he didn't snap in response. Instead, he leaned back against his chair, tapping a pencil on his desk.

It was Jean who spoke next, turning in her seat so she could look up at Helen. "They found out exactly what killed Eleanora. It was an ant poison. The sheriff showed up this morning with a warrant to search my house. He took that from my kitchen." She nodded toward Biddle's desk, and Helen noticed the bottle in the plastic bag set in front of him.

She let go of Jean and stepped closer. The sheriff didn't even make a noise of protest as she leaned over to squint at the bag's contents. "Splat?" she said, recognizing the bottle instantly. She glanced up at Biddle. "You're arresting her because of this?"

Biddle squirmed. "She isn't under arrest, Mrs. Evans," he said, "but the evidence is pretty incriminating. First," he ticked off on his fingers, "the poison was found in the goose liver she gave to Eleanora Duncan. Second, her fingerprints are the only ones on the container besides old Mrs. Duncan's and her housekeeper's. Third, she didn't get along with her former mother-in-law, as everyone in town knew. And finally, the poison in the pâté is a perfect match for this, which I found under her sink." He waggled a pinky at the bagged bottle. "It's loaded with sodium tetraborate. Though," he added almost grudgingly, "I did find the same insecticide under the sink at the Duncan house."

When Helen digested his final remark, she laughed out loud. "Good God, Sheriff, everyone in town uses Splat. The corner market sells it like hotcakes, just ask them. I bought a new bottle yesterday, and I certainly didn't kill Eleanora!"

Biddle ran a hand over his head, his frown deepening. "You're not a suspect, ma'am."

"Well, thank goodness for that." She crossed her arms over her breasts. "The paper says you've been questioning others connected to Eleanora. I hope that includes Floyd Baskin," she said, remembering something Zelma had mentioned the night Eleanora died. "Mr. Baskin was at the Duncan house earlier the day she was poisoned, wasn't he?"

Biddle sighed. "So it seems."

"Jemima Winthrop and Stanley Duncan also stopped by to see Eleanora that afternoon as well," Helen went on, because Zelma had told her that much, too.

The sheriff nodded but said nothing.

Helen shook her head, returning to stand beside Jean's chair. Her friend's expression had changed from one of anxiety to curiosity, as though she hadn't known about Eleanora's other visitors.

"If you're looking for someone who wanted Eleanora out of the way, why don't you start hounding Ms. Winthrop and Mr. Duncan instead of Jean," she suggested. "You might want to ask the two of them why they were meeting in secret at the playground last evening." Helen raised her eyebrows as she tacked on, "I don't think they were discussing the weather, do you?"

Biddle opened his mouth as if to retort but clamped it shut again.

Helen smiled tightly. "If you're not arresting Jean, you won't mind if I take her home, will you?"

The sheriff shot her a grumpy stare.

So Helen helped Jean up from her seat and hurried her toward the door before Biddle could change his mind.

To her surprise, he didn't come after them but merely called out, "Maybe Mrs. Duncan ought to call her lawyer. He might come in handy in the next day or so."

Helen briskly shut the door.

Chapter 16

HELEN REMAINED AT Jean's house just long enough to have a cup of coffee and make sure her friend was all right. Then she took off, walking toward the house on Harbor Drive that had—for as long as she'd lived in River Bend—belonged to the Winthrops. Despite losing so much in the bankruptcy auction, they had managed to hang out to that.

The stone and wood three-story structure sat but half a block away from the Duncans' home, yet they seemed miles apart in some respects.

Helen hadn't been inside the Winthrops' place in years, not since Reginald Winthrop had died. Before the patriarch's passing, the family had been one of the town's wealthiest, sponsoring the annual Fourth of July picnic and fireworks.

The house had been a wonder then, the lawns manicured, the shrubs pruned to perfection. The rosebushes surrounding the veranda had been breathtaking, blooming through the summers in every shade of red and pink one could imagine.

As Helen paused on the sidewalk at the foot of the driveway, she realized how long ago it had been since Reginald's death and how much had changed since.

Where the houses nearby had groomed yards and fresh paint, the Winthrops' looked sorely in need of a fresh coat. Every shutter was chipped and peeling, and the trim was blistered where it hadn't flaked off altogether.

The bushes in front were ill shaped and overgrown, and weeds poked their unsightly heads through bald patches in the grass.

Helen shook her head, finding the sight of it terribly sad. It was truly a reflection of what had happened to the Winthrops since Reginald's death.

It didn't surprise her that there was such bad blood between the Duncans and the Winthrops. As local gossip had it, Marvin Duncan had done more than simply buy the Winthrop granary out from under Reginald's feet. He'd used every dirty trick in the book to get Winthrop Grains into debt, then he'd bought the business for a song at auction and—if Helen remembered correctly—most of Reginald Winthrop's other assets as well, including the acreage near the harbor, family heirlooms, and antiques. Reginald Winthrop had started drinking heavily soon after and had died by his own hand from a mix of pills and a bottle of whiskey. His wife, Anna, had shut herself up in the house. Helen realized she couldn't recall the last time she'd seen her. Was she as bitter as her daughter? Did Anna also blame the Duncans for her family's misfortune?

Helen wondered what the truth really was or if anyone even remembered. Sometimes animosity caused such skewed perceptions that reality became buried beneath the angry stories.

She picked her way carefully across the cracked driveway before ascending the porch steps, which groaned and creaked unnervingly underfoot.

Before she rang the bell, she peered through the slim windows on either side of the door, but curtains barred her catching any glimpse inside.

Helen straightened her shoulders and pressed a finger to the doorbell. When she heard no chime, she raised the brass knocker and lay it down solidly several times.

After a minute had passed, she knocked with her fist. "Hello?" she said loudly, her cheek pressed into the dust on the door. "Is anyone home?"

She heard the slow tread of approaching feet before a timid voice asked, "Who's there?"

"Jemima, is that you? It's Helen Evans."

The lock clicked free.

The door came open but a sliver.

"Hello," Helen said, smiling, the tone one she'd used often to coax a stubborn grandchild from hiding beneath a bed. "I've come to see Jemima Winthrop. Is she here?"

An eye nearly hidden by crepelike skin studied her through a filmy pupil. A hint of white hair showed above, and Helen saw a hand on a cane below.

"Anna?" she blurted out, embarrassed for not recognizing the woman instantly. But then, Anna Winthrop was hardly as she remembered. "It's been a long time, hasn't it?"

The woman blinked her foggy eye before opening the door wider. For a long minute, she squinted at Helen. "You must have been a friend of Reggie's," she murmured, her voice soft and breathless. "I wasn't expecting anyone. Jemima isn't home, and I don't take visitors much. It isn't proper for a widow to entertain so soon after the funeral."

So soon after the funeral?

Helen didn't know what to say.

Reginald Winthrop had been dead for years. She was about to speak up and remind his widow of the fact, then she caught herself. The woman had dementia. It was no wonder Anna Winthrop left the house so rarely. "Do you know when Jemima will return?" Helen asked, uncertain of whether or not she'd get a lucid response.

Anna's crumpled face smiled. "I haven't a clue. She comes and goes. You know how these young girls are."

Jemima was sixty if she was a day.

"Yes, I do," Helen told her and nodded. She took a long look at Anna, noting the black dress she wore and the stoop of her back. She leaned heavily on the gold-tipped cane, as if she'd topple over without it. She looked a hundred or more, though she couldn't be more than, what, eighty? Helen figured she wasn't any older than Eleanora Duncan had been, anyway. That was just five years beyond Helen's own seventy-five. But, gazing at Anna, Helen felt like a spring chicken in comparison. Once the mind had gone, the rest of the body followed suit. Helen had seen it far too often.

"Where are my manners?" Anna said abruptly. "Land sakes, since you've come all this way, I should offer you a spot of tea at least. Would you like to come in, Mrs. Blevins?"

"It's Evans," Helen gently corrected.

"Of course it is," Anna said in her breathless way, her murky gaze drifting to Helen and then off in the distance. "Did you come by car? I should send someone out to fetch your bags?"

Helen played along again. "Oh, please, dear, don't bother. I don't want to trouble you further. I actually came to see Jemima, but since she's away, I'll try to catch her another time." She couldn't imagine Anna Winthrop boiling water, much less fixing the two of them a pot of tea.

"Did you forget your coat?" Anna asked. "You'll need it. It's rather chilly, isn't it?"

The day was near perfect, the temperature in the low seventies, but Helen noticed that Anna's humped shoulders had indeed begun to quiver.

"You do look cold," she said, "perhaps you should go back—"

"Just what the devil are you doing here?"

Helen hadn't heard anyone approach, and she started at the bark of the voice from behind her. She turned to find Jemima barreling up the steps, her dark eyes narrowed, her lips set in a line that carved deep furrows on either side of her mouth.

Helen put a hand to her heart. "Good heavens, but you startled me, sneaking around like that."

"I'd hardly call walking up to my own house 'sneaking around,'" Jemima countered and all but shoved Helen aside to reach her mother.

Anna gripped her cane and stared with unfocused eyes at her daughter. "Is that you, Jemmy?"

"Yes, Mama, it's me."

"Mrs. Melvin dropped by to pay her respects to your father," Anna said.

"Mrs. Melvin was just leaving," Jemima told her with one eye on Helen. "Why don't you go on inside, Mama? I'll be there in a minute."

Anna nodded blindly then slowly turned around, relying on the cane for support as she took one shuffling step after another.

As soon as she was out of the picture, Jemima pulled the door shut and faced Helen.

"My mother isn't well, Mrs. Evans, and she certainly doesn't need people like you bothering her."

"I didn't mean to do anything of the sort," Helen replied. "I stopped by to see you—"

"Me?" Jemima cut her off. "Why?"

"I suppose you've heard that Eleanora Duncan was poisoned."

Jemima planted her hands on her hips. "I also heard that the sheriff had Jean Duncan down in his office bright and early this morning. Did he arrest her?"

"No, he did not," Helen informed her. "Jean didn't have anything to do with Eleanora's murder."

"Didn't she now?" Jemima's thinly plucked eyebrows arched. "Don't get your knickers twisted, Mrs. Evans. I know Jean's your friend, and I don't blame her for what she did, not one little bit."

"She didn't do anything," Helen protested.

"Uh-huh."

Jemima looked pleased, her thin face wearing a smile that Helen thought better resembled a smirk. She could have been an attractive woman if not for the deep-set lines that ran from nose to mouth. Frown lines, Helen thought, and more telling of Jemima's bitterness than any words could have been.

"You really hated Eleanora, didn't you?" Helen said, watching the tug-of-war of emotions that played across Jemima's face. "All that pain the Duncans caused your family." She sighed and shook her head. "I can't say as I blame you."

Jemima whispered, "You don't know the half of it."

"I know more than you think," Helen told her. "For one, that you've been seeing Stanley Duncan in secret—"

"Please leave," Jemima snapped, not letting her finish, and her eye began to twitch. "I don't have time to listen to idle gossip."

She spun on her heel and disappeared inside.

The lock clicked.

The wind picked up suddenly, bringing with it a shot of cold, as though a dark cloud had washed over the sun. Helen rubbed her arms as she went down the porch steps and started walking along the drive. She made her way around a navy sedan covered with a fine layer of dust, and she shook her head, thinking her ears were going out on her. She hadn't even heard Jemima drive up.

With a sigh, she looked back at the Winthrop house and thought of Anna: each had seemed to age before her eyes.

Time had surely not been good to the Winthrops.

If Marvin Duncan had really been responsible for Reginald Winthrop's bankruptcy, it was no wonder Jemima hated Eleanora so much. But was that enough to have prompted her to put poison in Eleanora's pâté?

Ants must be bad this year, 'cause I've sold, like, a hundred bottles of the stuff this week alone. Miss Winthrop just bought her second batch in two days, would you believe.

Helen suddenly recalled the remarks of the checkout girl at the market, and she felt a growing sense of unease.

She drew in a deep breath, inhaling the muddy odor of the harbor, and she began to walk briskly, wanting to get as far away from the Winthrops' house as she possibly could.

Chapter 17

FRANK BIDDLE TRIED to concentrate on the reports from Eleanora Duncan's case file but found his mind wandering, and with good reason.

He'd read the contents at least ten times already, practically had the words memorized, and that included the list of food bagged from Eleanora Duncan's refrigerator. It was long enough to be mistaken for the inventory of a small grocery store. Frank closed his eyes and recited aloud, "One half gallon skim milk, organic prune and carrot juices, one jar of bread and butter pickles, a package of uncooked chicken breasts, pickled herring, and half a dozen pint-sized containers of cat food from a gourmet pet shop in Alton."

Oh, yes, plus the crab dip and stuffed mushrooms prepared by Jean Duncan, as well as the poisoned pâté.

Biddle sighed and pushed the case file away.

What if Eleanora Duncan had eaten the pâté when

Zelma hadn't been around to witness her stomach cramps and convulsions? If the old lady had been alone in the house when she'd died, no one would've been the wiser. No doubt it would've appeared she'd had a stroke or aneurysm or one of those other fatal medical terms he'd heard Doc mention.

Is that what Jean Duncan had hoped for? Had she figured Eleanora's death would be relatively quick and unquestioned? Had she assumed that the eighty-year-old widow would simply be buried without a fuss?

Surely she hadn't envisioned an autopsy.

He rubbed his eyes. He'd hardly slept last night. This case was getting to him, all right. He'd rolled over and reached for Sarah so he could wake her up and bounce some ideas around, but she hadn't been there.

"I'm staying a couple more days at my mother's, lamb chop, I hope you don't mind," she'd told him when she'd phoned a few minutes earlier. "Her hip replacement's been giving her trouble, so I'm going to the orthopedist with her in the morning. Though I do hope you miss me."

Frank thumped the heel of his hand against his chest and let out a belch that would've earned him applause in some kitchens.

Maybe Sarah was right about that cholesterol thing. He wasn't so sure that a few more days of eating at the diner wouldn't kill him.

That brought his thoughts right back to the murder.

Like the devil on his shoulder, Helen Evans's voice played in his head.

Why, just yesterday as I was leaving here, after Jean had

made up her mind to go to Eleanora's, she made a comment about hoping Eleanora wouldn't accuse her of trying to poison her. If that doesn't prove she's innocent, then I don't know what does. Why on earth would she say such a thing and then go poison her mother-in-law? That would be like pointing the finger at herself, wouldn't it?

Or perhaps it was a very clever way of deflecting guilt once Eleanora was dead.

But Mrs. Evans's voice didn't stop there.

Splat? You're arresting her because of this? . . . Everyone in town uses Splat. The corner market sells it like hotcakes.

Frank pressed his fingertips to his temples, as if the action would drive away the woman's persistent nagging. How he wished Mrs. Evans would just stay out of this!

He liked her. He really did. She was a nice enough lady with good intentions, and he admired her energy. She had enough of it to go around and then some. Hell, Frank could use some of it himself. Sarah was always dogging him about walking instead of driving the squad car everywhere he went. But he ranked exercise right up there with tofu and cleansing teas. Working up a sweat for no good reason just wasn't his style. He needed every ounce of energy to take care of the citizens of River Bend.

So he owed it to them to work on the case, not work out at a gym, he reasoned as he rubbed a hand over his weary face.

With a sigh, he reopened the file, placing it front and center on his desk, and attempted to look at it with fresh eyes. Okay, so what did he have here?

Eleanora was killed by a lethal dose of sodium tetraborate found in the goose liver pâté prepared by Jean Duncan. A bottle of Splat—the suspected poison—had been found in Jean Duncan's kitchen. Then there was the fact that Jean Duncan and her mother-in-law shared a deep, abiding hate.

So far as the sheriff was concerned, that gave the younger Mrs. Duncan motive, means, and opportunity.

That was a winning trifecta when it came to crimes like this.

So why hadn't he arrested Jean Duncan already? What was stopping him? The evidence was awfully obvious, but wasn't that the best kind? Simple cases were that much easier for prosecutors to explain to a jury, which usually meant a slam-dunk conviction.

If only Helen Evans's voice didn't keep popping into his brain.

If you're looking for someone who wanted Eleanora out of the way, why don't you start hounding Ms. Winthrop and Mr. Duncan instead of Jean? You might want to ask the two of them why they were meeting in secret at the playground last evening. I don't think they were discussing the weather, do you?

Damn it! There it was again.

Frank groaned loudly.

Why did such an otherwise lovely woman seem to believe she was Miss Marple incarnate?

Ah, well, he told himself, she was right about one thing anyhow. Jean Duncan might be the most obvious suspect, but she certainly wasn't the only one.

Frank had one eye on Floyd Baskin. The guy rubbed him entirely the wrong way. So Frank had put in a call to

Eleanora's lawyer and found out that yes, indeed, she had them working overtime, trying to put the kibosh on any further payments to the Save the River Fund. If Baskin knew about it, wasn't that motive for him to want Eleanora dead before she cut him off?

And then there was Stanley Duncan and Jemima Winthrop, suddenly a pair in the sheriff's mind since Mrs. Evans's report of witnessing their unlikely tryst.

Each had been at the Duncan house the day Eleanora had died, which meant both had had a chance to poison the pâté. Frank had found a bottle of Splat beneath the sink in Eleanora's kitchen. It would have been simple enough to hold the container of poison with a tissue so as not to leave behind any prints.

Frank's eyes began to blur and his head to ache. So he tapped the pages back into the manila file and put it away in his desk drawer. Then he rose from his chair.

The chimes of the carillon broke through the air, trilling out a clunky rendition of "My Old Kentucky Home," and Biddle found himself humming along with it.

So it was noon already, he realized, and his gut let out a grumble.

It wouldn't hurt any to go over to the diner and have lunch first. Investigating a murder was hard enough without having to do it on an empty stomach.

Chapter 18

THE OFFICE OF Save the River was just off Catfish Lane in nearby Grafton.

Helen guided her old Chevrolet into a spot on the graveled shoulder of the road, the river so near she could smell it.

She rounded a mud-splattered Ford with a SAVE THE RIVER bumper sticker, pausing on the sidewalk to take in the sight of Baskin's headquarters.

The place was little more than a shack—a wooden structure on cement blocks that kept it above water in the spring when the Mississippi ran over its banks.

She caught a glimpse of a rusted swing set in the dirt yard and figured it had once been someone's home, probably left behind after one too many floods. Baskin had likely gotten it for a song.

Well, it didn't pay to spend money on fancy digs when you were a charitable institution, right? In fact, Helen almost admired Baskin and his group for setting up space at such a low-rent site.

Almost.

After what she'd seen of Mr. Baskin yesterday, she didn't know if he'd be able to afford the lease another year, no matter how cheap.

Helen knew that Marvin Duncan had left money to Save the River. She'd heard it was an annual stipend or some such thing. If Eleanora had been as fed up with Baskin's tactics as the rest of River Bend was, maybe she'd tried to stop the flow of money. Was that why Baskin had stopped by to visit her the other day? Might the threat of losing such a reliable donation have driven him to murder?

Helen paused on the wooden steps. She held onto the decrepit railing and hesitated, recalling the rage she'd seen in Baskin's eyes as he'd spat at Clara Foley and ranted about giving them a taste of something toxic.

She swallowed as her mouth felt suddenly bone dry.

Is that what he'd done to Eleanora? Had he made her taste something so toxic she'd ended up dead?

Helen gripped the rail so tightly that she felt a prick.

"Ouch," she said and withdrew her hand. She held it away from her eyes and squinted at her palm, but everything looked too blurry.

She muttered under her breath and pulled her purse from the crook of her elbow, digging in it with her good hand to find her glasses, which she fast propped on her nose.

As she'd suspected, there it was.

The darned splinter was stuck right in the meatiest place at the base of her thumb. It was nice sized, too, plenty big enough to make its presence felt.

Maybe it was a warning, she thought. If she knew what was good for her, she'd turn around and leave. Instead, she ascended to the porch and, without so much as a knock on the door, turned the knob to find it unlocked.

She pushed her way inside.

"Hello?" she called. "Hello, can someone help me?"

The room was lit by old-fashioned fluorescent lights, and one of the bulbs flickered as if about to go out. Oversized maps of the region covered the knotty pine-planked walls. Each map had red-tipped pins stabbed into various places. A blackboard marked with dates and places hung above a nearby table. Picketing assignments? Or targets for more smoke bombs? Helen wondered. She noticed that River Bend's harbor had been written there and then crossed off. A utility plant in a town upriver seemed to be their next target. She wondered if she shouldn't warn the place.

"Have you been here long?" A thin girl in patched blue jeans emerged from the hallway. She tucked long yellow hair behind her ears. "Sorry, I didn't hear you come in. I was using the john."

The young woman didn't look a day over twenty, that age when cellulite and wrinkles seemed as distant as settlements on Mars. Her hazel eyes were wide and devoid of the dark liner and mascara that Helen saw on so many females these days, even tweens not old enough to drive. The T-shirt she wore had SAVE THE RIVER stamped on it. She smiled shyly at Helen's once-over, revealing slightly crooked teeth.

"My name's Lara. Can I do something for you?" she asked. She came nearer till Helen could see her bare feet. "Would you like to sign our petition demanding tighter regulations on dumping in the river? We're taking it to the governor ourselves, once we've got at least ten thousand names," she said, her eyes bright and skin flushed. "Or if you'd like, you can just make a donation. We take checks and all major credit cards, though cash is definitely okay, too."

If the girl hadn't been so incredibly earnest, Helen feared she might have laughed. But she swallowed back the tickle in her throat and, holding her injured hand palm up in the other, asked, "You wouldn't have a tweezers around here, would you? It appears that I caught a splinter outside on that railing of yours."

Lara blushed. "I keep telling Floyd we've got to move our office somewhere else, but he won't hear of it. Keeps telling me it's just where we answer our phones, not where we do our real work."

"Maybe Mr. Baskin is right."

"Sure he is," the girl said, her eyes lighting up. "Floyd's real smart about everything. He's got a bunch of college degrees," she added, gesturing at framed documents hanging crookedly above a desk. "He majored in chemical engineering, so he understands about sulfates and oxides and all the stuff people dump in the river." She smiled. "No one can pull anything over on Floyd."

The expression on her face was unmistakable. She's in love with Baskin, Helen thought, very nearly forgetting about the splinter. But not quite.

"A tweezers?" she reminded.

"Oh, yeah, sure," Lara mumbled, heading over to the desk and rummaging about in the drawers until she drew out a box of straight pins with colored heads. "Think this'd work?" she asked. "Sorry, it's the best I can do."

"Have you got some matches, too?"

The girl set aside the pins and managed to scrounge up a book of matches someone had swiped from a restaurant up the road.

Helen turned on the desk lamp, plucked a pin from the box, then struck a match and held it to the pin until the metal was singed black. Grimacing, she gingerly prodded until she worked the splinter out. Perhaps not the most sanitary of methods, but it did the trick.

"Oh, man, you're braver than I am," Lara went on. "I mean, I can't get blood drawn without practically passing out."

Helen looked at her and smiled. "By the time you're a grandmother, you won't have time to be squeamish. Now, if you'll excuse me, I need to wash up."

"Oh, sure, it's right back there." The girl pointed toward the hallway she'd emerged from a few minutes before.

Helen excused herself and went to wash her hands in the tiny lavatory. When she returned, the girl was sitting at the desk with a laptop opened before her.

"I don't mean to pry," Helen said, even though that was exactly what she meant to do, "but may I ask how long you've worked with Mr. Baskin? You do seem to be rather fond of him."

The hazel eyes locked on hers. "You're not here to make a donation, are you, Missus—"

"Evans," she said, "Helen Evans."

"Are you, Mrs. Evans?"

She pushed her purse up into the bend of her arm. "No, dear, I'm not. I'm trying to find out a few things about your friend Mr. Baskin."

"Like what?" Suspicion tightened the girl's voice.

"Well, he was pretty riled up yesterday when he led that protest at the harbor. Does he always get so angry?"

"What you call anger, I call passion," the girl defended. "What's so bad about that? Floyd would do anything for the cause, even if it means going to jail, which he has several times," she proudly added. "And if there was anything I could do to help him, well, all he'd have to do is ask." Her cheeks flushed, and she glanced at her lap.

Helen knew she wasn't going to get anything helpful from the young woman. There was no way Lara would utter a cross word about Baskin.

With a sigh, she turned to go, though she hesitated before she left, telling the girl, "Thank you for your help."

Then she closed the door on Lara's frowning face and left.

Chapter 19

"So ASK AWAY, Sheriff," Jemima Winthrop demanded, staring at Frank Biddle with a defensive look on her face. "You have questions for me about Eleanora Duncan. That is why you phoned and insisted I come down here, isn't it?"

"Yes, ma'am, and it shouldn't take long," he promised, hating how she had him feeling rattled. He flipped to a clean sheet of paper and held his pencil at the ready. "Where were you this past Monday morning?"

"Monday morning?" she repeated.

Frank watched her and waited.

Jemima touched her fingers to the single strand of pearls at her throat. "For God's sake, that was two whole days ago. I don't remember everywhere I went."

"Why don't you take a stab?" he said.

"I was p-probably at the library," she stammered and shifted in the chair until she suddenly came still. "Wait a minute, isn't that when someone tried to run down Eleanora? Are you trying to pin that on me?" She laughed, but the sound was brittle. "Look here, Sheriff," she said and leaned forward. "If I had attempted to flatten that old biddy like a squirrel on the road, I wouldn't have missed her. You'd still be scraping her off the pavement."

Whoa!

Frank realized his mouth was hanging open and promptly shut it, scribbling down nothing in particular but hoping to convince Jemima Winthrop otherwise. When he again felt composed, he ceased writing and glanced up to ask, "So, you don't have an alibi?"

She shrugged. "I *was* probably at the library, though Lord knows, I don't keep a journal of my whereabouts hour upon hour."

"Fair enough," the sheriff said and nodded. "What made you go see Eleanora that afternoon?"

Jemima sighed and fidgeted with her pocketbook. "Call me naïve, but I thought that nearly being run over may have softened up the old battle-axe so that she'd reconsider giving me back the land her husband stole from my family. It's the least she could do, after all."

"Stole?" Frank found her choice of words peculiar. "From what I heard, Marvin Duncan bought your father's assets on the auction block. There's nothing improper about that."

"That might be *how* it went, Sheriff, but that's not the whole of it," she insisted, and her cheeks flushed a most vivid pink. "As far as I'm concerned, Marvin and

Eleanora were thieves, first driving my father's company into debt so they could rip it out from under him, and then snatching away land that had been in my family for generations, not to mention treasures he and Mother had accumulated all their lives. They only managed to keep the house because Daddy had put it in trust to me. But that was little consolation to either of them. It's no wonder my father died so soon after. They took virtually everything he had. *Everything.*" Her hand gripped the armrests so fiercely that her knuckles turned white. "If you still want to call that proper, then you've a sick way of looking at it."

Her eyes did their best to pierce right through him, and Frank stuck a finger between his throat and collar, feeling suddenly as if the thermostat had been turned up to one hundred degrees.

The local gossips certainly had it right that Jemima had worked herself into a real lather over the Duncan family. Though Frank couldn't imagine a well-brought-up lady like Jemima shooting Eleanora or slitting her throat or clobbering her over the head—all rather messy forms of murder—he wasn't so sure about poison.

Poison was so much more ladylike.

Somehow, he could picture her at Eleanora's place, pacing about the kitchen as Zelma shuffled off to inform her mistress that she had an uninvited guest. In the meantime, Jemima had plenty of time to open up the fridge and withdraw the pâté. She could have brought Splat in her pocket—the bottle was tiny—and added a splash to the goose liver. Zelma's plodding footsteps would have given her ample warning to put everything back in its place.

"Sheriff, are you paying attention?" Jemima said shrilly. "Have you even heard a word I've said?"

Frank blinked away his thoughts. He cleared his throat and fixed his eyes on Jemima, who continued glaring at him and fingering her pearls. "I'm sorry, ma'am, I was distracted there for a minute. Please, continue."

The woman scowled, deepening the already hard lines etched into her skin. "I just wanted to know if you were through with me. I've a hundred other things to do this afternoon besides sit here while you amuse yourself."

Frank arched his eyebrows. Amuse himself? Did it look like he was playing a game of solitaire?

"Well, if you have nothing else to ask." She rose from the chair with a sniff, brushing at the pleats in her pants and slipping her purse over her shoulder. "Good day, Sheriff," she told him, and, chin up, she started off.

"Uh, ma'am, if you don't mind," Frank called to her back.

She hesitated halfway to the door. "What is it?"

"Just a few more questions, please," he said as kindly as he could.

She stomped back to the chair and settled down, only to begin a noisy tapping on the floor with the toe of her shoe.

The sheriff put aside his pencil and rested his forearms on his desk. "It sounds to me like you had a big enough beef with old Mrs. Duncan to want her dead. But maybe you didn't do it, at least not alone."

The thin line of her lips tightened until the skin around her mouth turned white. But she didn't say anything.

He scratched his forehead. "You mind telling me exactly why you were with Stanley Duncan last evening after dark? Mrs. Evans spotted the two of you together at the playground."

"Helen Evans is a certified busybody!" she snapped, her face reddening. "I told her once today already that whom I choose to meet and where I choose to meet them is nobody's business but my own."

Frank had to disagree. "When it comes to murder, ma'am, everything's my business."

Instead of explaining why she'd met with Stanley, Jemima crossed her arms and pursed her lips, saying nothing.

For one lingering moment, Frank found himself wishing all women could be like his wife. Sarah couldn't keep a secret to save her life. Unfortunately, it appeared that Jemima Winthrop could. He figured it'd be easier to pull an answer out of Stanley.

So he cleared his throat and moved on.

"One last thing, ma'am," he told her, ignoring her impatient snort, "I spoke with the salesgirl over at the corner market, and she tells me you bought several bottles of ant killer this week alone."

"Is that a crime?" Jemima asked.

"You do realize that Splat was used to kill old Mrs. Duncan?"

"Of course I do," she assured him. "The news is all over town. But that has nothing to do with me."

"The stuff is used so sparingly that two bottles seems like an awful lot of poison," Frank remarked, not about to let her squirm out of this one. "Do you have some kind of ant infestation?"

"So are you going to arrest me for buying too much Splat?" she said dryly. "I don't think there's a law against it, is there, Sheriff? Besides, we've had a terrible infestation at the library, so I keep a bottle there as well as at the house. You see, it's all perfectly innocent."

"Uh-huh," Frank murmured.

"You think I'm lying?" Her voice rose, and her face screwed up tighter. "Let me tell you something, Sheriff Biddle. If I'd wanted to kill Eleanora, I wouldn't have waited until Monday! I would have done it long ago, before I watched my father drink himself to death and my mother lose her mind!"

With that, Jemima jumped out of the chair and stormed out of the office.

Frank watched her go and shook his head.

"IF YOU THINK I'm going to confess to killing Eleanora, you're full of beans, Biddle," Stanley Duncan crabbed. "Pull any funny business, and I'll have my family's attorneys here quick as you can piss."

The sheriff was familiar with the Duncan family's attorneys. They were from a big firm in St. Louis and had more names on their letterhead than anybody could rightly remember.

Before Frank could get a word out, Stanley ranted on.

"I'd like to see you try and slap handcuffs on me," he growled. "I'll sue you if you do. Hell, I'll sue the whole town! Ever heard of false arrest or wrongful imprisonment or defamation of character? Take your pick!"

Honest to God, Frank was ready to strangle somebody with his bare hands.

He hunkered over his desk. The twinge of a headache that had started with Jemima Winthrop now blossomed into full-blown throbbing.

"Would you like to sit down?" he asked, not for the first time.

Stanley paced like a caged beast. Circling the room, stopping on occasion to poke a finger wildly in the air, he would holler, then resume his stalking.

"I'll say it again, I had nothing to do with murdering my sister-in-law, although I won't lie and tell you I'm torn up about her death," Stanley told him. "She made my life miserable, she did. She took what was rightfully mine and kept it from me all these years."

Frank squinted at the man, pegging him to be about middle to late sixties. Erma at the diner had mentioned the younger of the Duncan brothers had left home at twenty, only returning on occasion for brief visits. "Stan had ants in his pants," was how Erma had put it. "He wanted to travel and see the world. But he didn't want to work. He wanted the good life, like his brother, only that's harder to do when your pockets are empty."

Stanley finally ceased pacing and marched up to Frank's desk, bending his tall body over it. "You can't have a shred of evidence that connects me to what happened to Eleanora. Not a shred."

The sheriff sighed. "Look, I'm not arresting you, Mr. Duncan, I just want to ask a few questions." *If you'd ever shut up,* he left unsaid.

Stanley straightened up. He ran a hand over a full head of gray hair that caused Frank a pang of envy. "A few questions, you say?"

Biddle nodded. "It won't take long," he said, and it was an easy promise to make, what with the way his head banged.

"I guess I can spare a minute."

"Much appreciated."

Reluctantly, Stanley settled into a wooden chair and set his elbows on his knees. He rubbed his hands together, either because he was cold or he couldn't keep them still.

Frank picked up his pencil and flipped to a clean page on his pad. "Have you been in town long, Mr. Duncan?"

"Oh, not more than a week, I guess. I'm staying in Grafton at a B&B." A faint smile tugged at his lips. "I might have to stick around longer than I figured, what with me being the only Duncan still standing." He nodded to himself. "I'm counting on moving into the house on Harbor as soon as the will is read."

The sheriff cocked his head. "You seem awfully sure of that."

Stanley shrugged. "I can't imagine anything happening otherwise. Who else is there? Eleanora would have had to be off her rocker to leave the place to that antique who calls herself a housekeeper."

"What about Jean?" Frank asked.

"Are you kidding me, Biddle? Eleanora leave anything to Jean?" Stanley laughed. "I was going to say over Eleanora's dead body, but that's the case now, isn't it?" He shook his head. "I guarantee you, Jean is getting nothing."

The sheriff had another question itching to be asked. "So you were in River Bend on Monday morning?"

Stanley patted his knees. "I guess I was at that."

"Do you have a car?"

"When I need one, I've got one to borrow" was all he said.

Frank made a note then tapped the pencil against his chin. "When you're not in town, where do you live?"

"Live?" Stanley grinned. "Why, the world is my oyster, Biddle."

"How do you survive?"

"I do this and that. I once sold real estate, but that wasn't my cup of tea. Even did some bookkeeping that didn't last. It's insane how bookkeepers get blamed for every damned cent that goes missing." Stanley glanced around the room. "I did a little telemarketing, you know, pushing gold bullions, and I tried my hand at selling cars. But nothing stuck." He flashed Frank a toothy grin. "Guess I'm just not cut out for that nine-to-five stuff."

"Why didn't you stick around and work for Duncan Industries?"

The man's faced clouded, his eyebrows knitting together. "Eleanora always had a big influence on Marvin. She could've talked my brother into jumping off the Eads Bridge if she'd had a mind to. She never wanted me to stick around. Besides"—he sighed and wiggled a hand in the air—"I could never get myself worked up over grain and silos and subsidies. I played right into her hands, though, didn't I, by staying away?"

For the moment, Frank forgot about his headache. "You really didn't like your sister-in-law, did you, Mr. Duncan?"

"Are you serious? The old girl was a pain in the—" He stopped midsentence, eyeing Biddle with suspicion. "You're trying to get me to say something I'm going to regret, aren't you?" He got up abruptly and brushed off his pants. "Well, you can forget it, Biddle. It won't happen, not with me. Besides, you're barking up the wrong tree." He approached Frank's desk and leaned over, looking him squarely in the face. "Jean's the one who killed her. And even if Eleanora lost her head and wrote Jean into her will, I know for a fact that a murderer can't inherit from her victim. So it looks like I've got a clear shot of finally getting all that's mine."

He turned and started for the door.

The sheriff scrambled to his feet. "Mr. Duncan?"

Stanley turned around. "Yes?"

"Do you mind telling me what's going on between you and Miss Winthrop?"

"Me and Jemmy?" Stanley lifted his shoulders then dropped them. "I hardly know the woman, Sheriff," he said. Then he left, closing the door with a clatter.

Frank got up from his desk and walked to the window. He watched Stanley cross the street toward the diner.

So he hardly knew "Jemmy," did he?

Right.

Frank sighed. Could Mrs. Evans be onto something? Were Stanley Duncan and Jemima Winthrop in cahoots?

The mere thought made the hammering in his head even worse.

Chapter 20

HELEN HAD WANTED to call off the weekly bridge game
already pushed from Tuesday night to Wednesday, but her
friends wouldn't hear of it.

"My word, Helen," Clara Foley had protested. "The
world hasn't come to a standstill. I don't mean to sound
callous, but don't you imagine Eleanora Duncan would've
gone on about her life if one of us had been poisoned? I
doubt she'd have even noticed, to tell you the truth, way
over there on Harbor Drive in that ivory tower of hers."

Maybe so, but Helen still didn't feel like it was in good
taste to play cards with Eleanora not even buried, Jean on
the hook, and the real murderer running loose.

Clara had laughed when she'd said as much. "Well, it's
not like her killer's going to show up and cut the deck."

Or maybe her killer would do exactly that, Helen
thought as she looked over the hand she'd been dealt,
staring past Clara Foley's topknot to the next table, where

Jemima Winthrop sat opposite Bertha Beaner. Bertha hadn't told her the name of the sub she'd found for Sarah Biddle, and Helen knew why.

Jemima glanced up from her hand, and Helen quickly ducked her chin.

"I bid a heart," Clara Foley announced, the flesh of her cheeks dimpling several times over. The bright yellow of her caftan lent her the appearance of an overfed canary.

Fanny Melville sighed. "Well, I'm beginning to wonder if the deck's not stacked, the way the cards are turning in your favor. You got 'em marked or something, Helen?"

"What?" She heard her name but missed the question. "Sorry, dear, I wasn't listening."

Fanny gazed at her over the rims of her spectacles. "It's amazing how you manage to keep winning, what with your mind a million miles away. You must be on automatic pilot."

Helen smiled, feeling a little sheepish for not paying better attention to the game.

"I hate to do it." Doc's wife sighed and slapped her cards facedown on the table. "But I'll have to pass."

Clara giggled and started to hum the Michigan fight song under her breath.

Helen ignored her, studying her hand. Fanny was right. The tide did seem to have turned in their favor. "I bid a spade," she said.

Verna Mabry, in a lime green sheath with a cloche hat to match, sniffed loudly. "Good God, I almost think we should quit now and cut our losses, eh, Fanny?"

Her partner chuckled. "Well, we each did throw a

quarter in the pot tonight, didn't we?" She put a finger to her chin and rolled up her eyes as if in deep thought. Then she waved a hand in the air. "Aw, go on, Verna. Fifty cents won't break us."

The LCIL president's taut face frowned. "Pass," she said.

And around again they went.

The murmur of voices from the two tables filled the screened-in porch, though the noise they made was a shade less than when there were three tables. But they were five players short tonight, what with Sarah Biddle still out of town, Bebe Horn sick with the flu, Lola Mueller babysitting her grandson, and Agnes March at an antiques auction in the city.

And Jean was missing, too, Helen mused, scrunching up her brow as she remembered how shaken the poor dear had been after Frank Biddle had hauled her downtown this morning. Why, Jean had imagined she was about to be tossed behind bars, and it was no wonder she wasn't in the mood for a few hands of bridge.

"It's too bad about Jean, isn't it?"

She looked up at the mention, hearing Verna's voice, feeling as if she'd been thinking too loudly.

"What's that?" she asked, fixing her eyes on her friend.

Verna waved manicured fingers. "It's just that I can't believe it was Jean's pâté that was poisoned. I hardly think that'll do much for her fledgling catering business, do you? Everyone's heard about it, and now they're all squawking at me to find someone else to do the food for the luncheon." The tendons at her neck tightened. "I suppose I should wait to see if she's actually charged with the murder before finding another caterer. But I'd hate to put it off too long and get stuck without anyone. Then I'd have to break down and call the Catfish Barn."

"Oh, God," Clara groaned. "Talk about poison!"

Helen couldn't listen to another word. "Stop acting like the worst is going to happen," she said more snippily than she'd meant to. "Jean's not going to be charged with murder. She didn't kill Eleanora."

Verna tipped her lime-topped head. "I know you're great friends with her and all, and I've nothing against her myself. But really, Helen, how can you be so sure?"

"I hate to say it," Fanny Melville added, "but sometimes even people we think we know the best turn out to be strangers. Everyone has their breaking point."

"Especially considering how Eleanora treated her," Clara Foley chimed in. "The woman acted like Jean murdered Jim, as if she'd run her car off the road on purpose."

"Enough!" Helen smacked down her cards, earning her a trio of surprised stares. She felt embarrassed suddenly, knowing they hadn't meant any harm with their gossip; they were just rattling on as they always did. She drew in a deep breath and slowly exhaled. Then she smiled weakly and picked up her hand. "Let's get back to the game and save the chitchat for later?"

"Okey dokey," Clara murmured.

"Sure," Fanny and Verna said, exchanging looks.

Helen nodded at them.

Fanny peered over her bifocals and asked, "Where were we?"

"It's my turn, so look out." Clara squirmed, and the wicker chair crackled beneath her. "Two hearts," she said in a rush.

"Pass," Fanny muttered.

Helen didn't hesitate. "Four hearts," she said.

Verna groaned. "Well, Fanny, I think you were right. Maybe we should just throw in the towel before they completely embarrass us."

"You're almost making me feel sorry for you," Clara said with a chuckle. "What're you angling for, a sympathy card?" She laughed at her own joke.

But Verna shushed her and leaned in. "That reminds me, girls. Mildred Masters, a friend of mine whose husband works at Hartford, Martin, Dervish, and Lynch in St. Louis, told me something interesting." Her ever-wide eyes darted from one face to another. "Anyone who subscribes to the *River Bend Bulletin* online will be getting an email in the morning about it, but I'll give you a heads-up. It concerns Eleanora—"

"Didn't you just agree not to talk about the murder?" Helen cut her off, not wanting to hear another word about whether or not Jean poisoned her mother-in-law.

"But, Helen, it's not bad news, and it has nothing to do with Jean," Verna promised. "It's about a party for Eleanora."

Clara let out a guffaw. "You sure you didn't have your brain tucked with that last face-lift, sweetie? Eleanora's dead, remember?"

"My brain is fine," Verna replied with a sniff and absently patted her cheeks. "The party is part of Eleanora's will. She left instructions that there be some kind of celebration when she kicked the bucket. I don't know all the details, but it sounds like Lady Godiva is the hostess."

"The dead woman's cat," Fanny murmured, echoing Helen's very thoughts. "That's quite unusual, to say the least."

"It's wacky is what it is," Clara insisted.

"Where will this party be held?" Helen asked.

"Girls, please, I don't know all the details," Verna said with a roll of her eyes. "We'll just have to check our email boxes in the morning. All Mildred knew was that Eleanora's will stated in black and white that she wanted a party, not a funeral. And there's no sense waiting on a party, since they don't need the sheriff or the medical examiner's permission to throw a shindig."

"Particularly one hosted by a cat," Helen murmured, finding it very strange indeed.

She couldn't help but glance at Jemima Winthrop and wonder if Eleanora's killer would be attending.

Chapter 21

HELEN WASN'T A very good geek. She considered herself a dinosaur in an age of high-tech gadgets. So although she did like Skyping with her grandkids on occasion, she didn't religiously check her computer for email every day.

But on that Thursday morning after bridge club, Helen got online soon after waking. She checked for the email invitation that Verna Mabry had mentioned, but she didn't see it in her in-box or stuck amidst her spam.

She fed Amber breakfast and chewed on a piece of toast with raspberry jam then looked for the email again afterward, finally finding precisely what she'd been waiting for.

The subject header read: In Celebration of Eleanora Duncan. The body of the email explained the details.

Please join Lady Godiva to honor the life of her dearly departed mother at River Bend Town Hall today at noon. Cake and punch provided. A donation of cash, a toy, or pet food for the Animal Rescue Fund is required for entry.

Do come and help celebrate Eleanora's generous spirit and love of creatures of all kinds.

Helen noted the Do Not Reply to the Email message, so there was no way to RSVP. She guessed the Duncan family's lawyers were figuring that whoever showed up showed up, and whoever didn't, fine.

A party hosted by a feline for her deceased mommy.

Hmm, Helen thought. She'd lived long enough to have seen and heard almost everything, but this was a first. And still she knew she wouldn't miss it for the world.

THE TOWN HALL was packed to the gills. So crowded, in fact, that Helen had to wait in line to enter, and she'd arrived precisely at noon.

So she stood on the sidewalk clutching a plastic bag full of canned cat food. It was the Liver 'n' Chicken that Amber had loved last week but rejected this week. Somehow, she doubted that dogs were anywhere near as fickle as cats.

"Howdy, Helen," Clara Foley said as she ambled up and took a place in line behind her. "Can you believe this? I'm having flashbacks of buying Cabbage Patch dolls for my kids."

Helen shook her head, gazing at the growing line behind them and the crush of bodies they could see through the open front door.

"I didn't know this many people even subscribed to the *River Bend Bulletin*," Clara added and hugged a bag of doggy kibbles to her breasts.

When they finally got to the door, a smartly dressed woman greeted them with a smile, took their donations, and gave them a pair of party hats.

Above them, colorful paper streamers crisscrossed the ceiling. Pots of vibrant flowers sat on tabletops. Amidst it all were countless photographs of Eleanora with Lady Godiva.

"So there you are!" Fanny Melville squeezed through the press of bodies to find them. Helen smiled at the sight of the polka-dotted hat perched atop her gray head, the ever-present spectacles sitting on her nose. "Oh, Lord, you have to see the cake," Doc's wife said, taking Helen's hand and attempting to drag her through the crush. "There's a giant photo of Lady Godiva and Eleanora painted in the frosting."

Clara came along, and the three of them traipsed toward the refreshment table across the room. Helen spotted a hatless Sheriff Biddle, his sparse hair neatly brushed across his pate. She saw Jemima Winthrop looking like she was dressed for a garden party in a floral dress and yellow hat.

"They have punch in crystal bowls with strawberries in big chunks of ice," Fanny was saying, hanging onto Helen's hand so she didn't lose her.

Was that Floyd Baskin with the young woman, Lara, from Save the River? Helen couldn't believe they'd had the nerve to come any more than Jemima had.

Finally they reached their destination and Fanny let go of her hand.

"You'd better take a look," Doc's wife said, "before they

start cutting Lady Godiva and her dearly departed mother into little pieces."

"Oh, my heavens," Helen breathed, and Clara let out a low whistle over her shoulder.

The cake was enormous, nearly as large as the table itself. Fanny hadn't lied. The colored frosting depicted Eleanora hugging a pug-faced Lady Godiva. Helen had never seen such a happy smile on Eleanora's face, at least not since Marvin and Jim had died.

"Let's get some punch before they're out," Fanny said over the loud chatter around them. Clara piped up, "I'll help."

Helen stared at the frosting photo and wondered what her children and grandchildren would think if she wrote in her will that they should throw her a party with an obscenely large cake depicting her holding Amber. They'd probably figure she'd lost her marbles.

"This isn't right," she heard a voice mutter from beside her, and Helen realized Zelma Burdine had quietly appeared on her left. "It's just not right," she said again and picked up the shiny silver cake knife set on the edge of the table.

"Oh, Zelma," Helen said, seeing the woman's tearful face. Her eyes were saggy and shadowed, like she'd hardly slept in days. "How are you faring?" she asked, though the answer was apparent.

"She had a husband and a son," Zelma said, as if she hadn't heard Helen's question. "And when she lost them, there were still people who loved her. But all that seemed to matter was the cat."

The woman sniffled, and Helen touched her arm. "Grief is a terrible thing," she remarked. "Eleanora lost so much. I guess she needed Lady Godiva to fill that empty spot in her heart."

"But she had me, too," Zelma whispered, and, without warning, she brought the fat knife down into the cake, reaching as far as she could to cut a line down the painted frosting right between Eleanora and Lady.

Just then, Fanny and Clara jostled their way over. Doc's wife pushed a cup of frothy pink punch into Helen's hand.

"Oh, Zelma, are you cutting the cake already?" Clara asked, only to be interrupted by Fanny Melville bursting out, "My God, Helen, you have to see the setup in front. They've got Lady Godiva on a chair that looks like a throne."

Helen looked away from Zelma slicing up the cake and caught sight of Stanley Duncan, chatting up the mayor. She frowned. Surely he didn't subscribe to the *River Bend Bulletin*, too?

"This way," Fanny urged, setting down her punch cup to grab hold of Helen. With Clara on their heels, the trio pushed their way toward Lady's throne.

Helen could just see the high ornate back of a chair placed in front, where Art Beaner normally stood at the podium during town hall meetings. They were nearly close enough for her to glimpse Lady without standing on her toes, when something shifted around her. The atmosphere changed. People stopped talking. Everyone seemed to stand still.

Helen smacked right into Fanny's backside, and half her punch splashed out of her cup onto her shoes. It was a good thing she'd worn pink Keds. At least they matched the punch.

When she looked over to see what had caused all the commotion—or rather, the lack of commotion—a lump caught in her throat.

Jean Duncan strode into the mix with her head held high, her silver hair tied back neatly in a black scarf. She had on black jeans and a black twinset as well, pearls at her throat. She was the only one in the room dressed for a casual funeral rather than a death party with a kitty hostess.

"What's she doing here?" Stanley Duncan's voice rose, and a ripple of whispers followed suit. "Someone throw her out!"

"Jean," Helen said as her friend came near, but Jean looked right past her.

Eleanora's daughter-in-law headed straight toward the giant cake. Was she going to deface it? Helen wondered. But it was Zelma that Jean was aiming for.

The housekeeper let out a sputter cry of "Oh, you came! Someone does care," she said and began to wail.

Stanley Duncan quit shouting for the sheriff to drag Jean out. Indeed, no one said anything as Zelma cried her heart out against Jean's chest.

Helen's heart lurched, hearing such gut-wrenching sobs.

At least Zelma's grief was real enough, she thought and looked over at Stanley and then across the way at

Jemima. Although soon after, Jemima's yellow hat began to bob through the crowd and then vanished altogether. Helen looked around to see where Jemima had gone and realized Stanley Duncan seemed to have disappeared as well.

"Thank you all for coming today," a clear voice said through the room's speakers, and Helen noticed the pretty woman from the law firm who'd been gathering up the donations. She now stood up front beside the intricately carved chair.

Helen popped up on tiptoes to see Lady Godiva slumbering on a purple cushion, seeming not to care that the room was full of humans. Or perhaps she was depressed, grieving for Eleanora.

As the pretty lawyer droned on about Eleanora's generosity and dedication to causes of all stripes, Helen found her mind drifting off.

She thought of Monday morning, when she'd gone out for a walk, and how she'd witnessed Lady Godiva chase a butterfly into the middle of Harbor Drive. Then Eleanora had stepped into the road, an engine had gunned, tires squealing as a car had driven right toward her as though it had meant to mow her down.

What if she hadn't been there to pull Eleanora from its path? Helen's heart pounded faster. She was sure that Eleanora would have been killed. Had the killer failed, only to succeed a second time with poison?

Helen closed her eyes and tried to recall what the car had looked like, but all she came up with were those things she'd told Biddle: it had been an older model sedan of some dark hue, maybe blue, maybe brown.

Jemima Winthrop drove a navy four-door.

She'd seen Stanley Duncan tooling about River Bend the past few days in a muddy late-model Lincoln.

And she remembered another brown sedan parked out front of the Save the River office in Grafton. Did it belong to Floyd Baskin or his girlfriend?

She turned at the sound of Zelma's sobs and saw Jean still there, her arm wrapped around the crying woman. Helen's throat tightened as she realized Jean owned a gray Buick.

I think somebody's trying to kill me.

Those were Eleanora's very words, as if she'd had some cause to suspect the worst. Had she been getting threats? Had an attempt been made on her life before that?

Helen had asked Zelma that very thing, but the housekeeper had said she couldn't recall anything of the sort.

Helen let out a loud sigh, and Clara nudged her with an elbow.

Though she tried to focus on the perky lawyer babbling about Eleanora's goodness, Helen's mind drifted again. There was too much clouding her brain.

She flashed back to Jean's smiling face. Oh, how happy she'd been at starting up her catering service. Why would she have risked it all just to be rid of Eleanora? Would it have been worth so much to her to have her mother-in-law out of her life forever?

The poison had been in Jean's pâté.

The only fingerprints on the container belonged to Jean, Eleanora, and the housekeeper. Biddle had found a bottle of Splat in Jean's kitchen, though admittedly one had been under Eleanora's sink.

It all seemed so neat, almost too neat. If a bow had been tied around the evidence, it wouldn't have appeared any more perfectly presented.

Was Jean being framed? she wondered. Everyone in town knew Jean hated Eleanora. But how had the murderer set it all up?

Helen had only heard about Jean's new business venture from Jean herself the morning that Eleanora died. At that point, it wasn't common knowledge. Who else could have realized the plastic container labeled The Catery was from Jean's kitchen? Unless Zelma had let it slip that Jean had delivered the items or the murderer had looked up Jean's newly-created web site.

There had been other food in the refrigerator. Why had the pâté been poisoned and nothing else? Biddle hadn't mentioned sodium tetraborate being found in anything but the goose liver. So had the murderer intentionally poisoned the delicacy rather than, say, a jar of pickles?

What was she missing? Helen tapped a finger to her chin. The answer was there, she knew it. But the more she tried to figure things out, the more frustrated she got.

No wonder Biddle had lost so much hair.

"Lady Godiva was very special to Eleanora," the pretty lawyer was saying and picked up the ball of fur from the throne. She held the cat high, as if on display. Lady mewed and took a swipe at her. "Lady Godiva inspired Eleanora to sit on the board of numerous animal rescue operations across the county. She hoped that all creatures, great and small, would find homes and be loved as much as she loved her precious baby."

Lady let out another mew, but it was drowned out by a human howl.

Helen swiveled her head to see an unsmiling Jean trying hard to console a desolate Zelma. The poor dear bent like a hunchback, sobbing into Jean's sweater.

What would happen to Zelma? Helen wondered. Where would she go? What about the house on Harbor Drive? Would that dreadful brother of Marvin's get everything? Who would take care of Lady Godiva?

Helen murmured, "Excuse me a minute," to Clara and Fanny, then she made her way toward Jean and Zelma.

"Can I do anything to help?" she asked and set down her half-empty cup of punch. She glanced sideways at the cake to see that Zelma had done quite an interesting job of cutting it up. It looked very much like she'd dissected Lady Godiva and Eleanora both.

This time, Jean didn't look through her. Her friend's pale eyes met hers. "Could you wet a towel with cold water? I think Zelma needs to sit down and cool off."

"Of course," Helen said, knowing there were all sorts of embroidered tea towels stocked in the powder rooms of town hall. She'd made half of them herself. "I'll be right back."

She maneuvered toward the back hallway, then to her right, where a pair of doors were marked LADIES and GEN-TLEMEN, although both bathrooms were exactly the same, with a pedestal sink, toilet, mirror, and trash can. The only difference was their colors—pink for girls and blue for boys—and the fact that the ladies' room door never seemed to properly lock.

Helen grabbed the knob, which easily turned. She pulled open the door to the restroom painted Pepto-Bismol pink, flipped on the ceiling light, and found Stanley Duncan and Jemima Winthrop embracing.

Chapter 22

THE PAIR PULLED apart as fast as they were able. Jemima smoothed down her dress and righted her yellow hat, which had been knocked cockeyed. Stanley wiped the back of his hand across his mouth, though he still wore a trace of lipstick on his upper lip.

"My word, woman, haven't you ever thought to knock?" he growled.

Helen simply stared.

Jemima fingered her pearls. "I just came in to use the restroom, and I happened to bump into Stanley . . . uh, Mr. Duncan."

I'll say she did, Helen mused. She bumped into him so hard their lips locked.

"Well, I, uh, was just leaving," Jemima murmured after composing herself. "So if you'd excuse me."

Jemima came forward and tried to sidestep her, but

Helen backed up to the door. She put her hand on the knob. "I think it'd be a good idea if you both just stayed put. I imagine the sheriff would like the chance to find out what's really going on between you. I know I'm curious myself."

Stanley and Jemima exchanged glances.

The knob rattled then turned. Helen felt the door nudge open and quickly stepped out of its path.

"What's going on?" Jean looked into the room, the frustration on her face changing to confusion. "Zelma got herself so worked up she fainted. Fanny Melville's got some smelling salts out, but I should really take her home." She glanced at Helen though her eyes kept flickering back to Stanley and Jemima. "I figured you'd want to know."

"I'm sorry I was so slow," Helen said. "But something besides the tea towels caught my eye."

Jemima's head reared, and suddenly she appeared more like her old self. "Why, you're not going to *tell* her, are you?" Her voice crackled. She crossed her arms over her breasts, the floral silk of her dress swaying with her indignation. "Of all the people . . . it would have to be you who butted your nose in where it didn't belong." She swiveled to Stanley. "She's got the biggest mouth in town! She'll twist everything all around, and by the time it gets to the sheriff's ears, he'll be ready to slap us in handcuffs!"

Helen blinked, trying not to take offense at the remark, considering the source. Jemima Winthrop was more than likely a murderer, or at least an accomplice. Compared to that, being called a gossip didn't seem so awful.

"Hey, none of this is my fault," Stanley countered. "You're the one who wants to hook up in the strangest places."

"Me?" Jemima shot back. "Well, you're the one who couldn't bear to wait another minute to put your paws all over me."

"Hey, don't go acting shy now, when you were the one who came after me like a cougar in heat."

"A cougar in heat?" Jemima repeated, looking truly pissed off.

"You heard me," Stanley told her.

"How could I not, the way you're yelling."

"*I'm* yelling? Of all the crazy . . . "

Helen felt as if she were watching Wimbledon, with the ball going back and forth, back and forth.

Jean stood in the doorway, wide-eyed. Her face was white as ash.

"What in tarnation is all this shouting?" Helen heard the sheriff sputter. Jean moved out of the way, and Frank Biddle entered the powder room.

"Ah, Mrs. Evans," he said, like that explained everything, and Helen pointed at Jemima and Stanley, who still argued, nose to nose.

"I caught them red-handed," she said before adding, "in a clench."

"You don't say?" The sheriff hiked up his belt. "Break it up," he said as the pair continued to squabble. "Enough's enough." Biddle firmly moved Helen aside to reach Jemima and Stanley. He separated them, stepping in the middle like a boxing official stopping a fight.

"You ass," Jemima said, and Helen couldn't tell if she meant Biddle or Stanley.

"Crazy woman," Stanley shot back, hoping he didn't mean her.

They both crossed their arms and glared.

Biddle shook his head at them before he fixed his gaze on Helen. He sighed loudly. "Okay, Mrs. Evans, want to tell me what you've started now?"

Helen resisted the urge to say something she might regret. Instead, she jerked her chin at Jemima and Stanley. "There's something going on between them, all right, just as I told you. When I walked in, I saw the two of them kissing."

"Busybody," Jemima whispered but pressed her lips tight again.

Stanley shifted on his feet.

"You're so focused on Jean that you can't see what's right under your nose," Helen told Biddle, gesturing at Jean, who lingered near the door. "These two have some explaining to do, Sheriff, don't you think? For all we know, they murdered Eleanora and painted Jean as the prime suspect! Why else would they hide their relationship?"

Biddle cleared his throat, glancing from Jemima to Stanley. "She's got a point, you know. I'd like to hear what the both of you have to say."

"Are you arresting us, Sheriff?" Stanley spoke out first. "If that's the case, let me step into the other room and get my lawyer. That pretty young thing works for the Duncan family, you know."

"Why don't you can it, Stan?" Jemima blurted out. "It's time to spill."

"But, Jemmy, you said that we had to keep on the down low—"

"I'm done with sneaking around," she cut him off. "Don't you get the picture? If we don't tell the truth, the whole town's going to think we murdered Eleanora. Mrs. Evans will make sure of it." She gave Helen the stink eye.

Helen didn't even flinch. "Did you kill Eleanora?"

"I certainly didn't poison the old biddy," Stanley said.

"And neither did I," Jemima chimed in. "No matter what anyone thinks," she added, looking directly at Helen. Then Jemima reached for Stanley's hand and held it, her face softening. "We've been seeing each other for years, if you must know. I'd usually have to go meet him somewhere outside of town. It was too risky being seen together around here, especially with the bad blood between our families." She hesitated. "I couldn't take the chance of anyone finding out we'd gotten married."

"Married?" Helen caught her breath.

Jean slipped inside the doorway, hands on her cheeks. "How?" she asked. "When?"

Jemima didn't take her eyes off Stanley as she answered, "We saw a justice of the peace a week ago. That's why Stanley came back. He said he wanted to talk to Eleanora about getting his mother's wedding ring. Marvin had always promised he could have it if he ever found anyone worthy of settling down."

Was that why he'd been in Eleanora's house the other day, tearing the place apart? Helen wondered. Zelma had thought he was looking for money, but all he'd mentioned was wanting "what was mine."

"I didn't want my mother to know," Jemima went on, a catch in her voice. "I couldn't risk pushing her even further into madness. She's living on the brink as it is, sometimes lucid and sometimes . . ." She sighed. "I was afraid that knowing Stanley and I were together would kill her, and I'd already lost Daddy to the Duncans." She peered at Helen from beneath her hat's yellow brim. "You saw what a fragile state she's in. If she even heard mention of Eleanora, it sent her spiraling downward."

And there's the rub, Helen thought, speaking up. "So if Eleanora was out of the way, you two could stop sneaking around?"

Jemima's eyes went wide. "I never said that!"

"Were you figuring, too," Helen went on, "that Stanley would inherit the Duncan fortune? Then he could return to you what you've always believed Marvin and Eleanora stole from your family, including that acreage by the harbor you want for a new library. With the way prices of real estate have gone up around here lately, it's probably worth a pretty penny."

"Stop it, no!" Jemima cried out. "No, that's not it! I mean, we discussed the fact that Stanley might inherit something, but we never talked of killing her. We just had to be patient."

"Yes, patient," Stanley echoed and squeezed Jemima's hand.

But Helen didn't buy a word of it.

"Jean? Jean, where did you go?" A soft voice preceded the shuffle of footsteps, and Zelma was at the door, her cheeks red and tear-streaked. Behind the huge Coke bottle glasses, her tiny eyes appeared puffy and pink. "I want to go home," she mewled.

"Yes, of course," Jean said and took her arm.

"I'll drive you," the sheriff said and headed out after them.

Helen couldn't believe he was leaving Jemima and Stanley and not hauling them down to the station! She dogged his footsteps, telling him, "If I were you, Frank Biddle, I'd strongly take Eleanora's will into consideration. With so much money involved, as well as control of Duncan Industries, there's plenty of cause for those two to poison Eleanora. Why, even if they counted on Stanley receiving just a fraction, it's good enough reason for murder in my book."

Why was he shaking his head, for heaven's sake?

"The money trail," Helen said, not letting go. "Can't you see where it leads?"

He stopped in his tracks and turned around. Jean and Zelma did the same.

"It doesn't lead to them," he said, looking smugly at Helen. "I spoke with Eleanora Duncan's lawyers this morning."

Stanley and Jemima emerged from the powder room in time enough to catch Biddle saying, "Stanley Duncan isn't a beneficiary. No one is, not an actual person, anyway."

"What are you talking about?" Stanley snapped. "I'm

the only surviving Duncan! The old bat must've left me something."

Jemima cocked her head, crooking her yellow hat.

Jean clutched Zelma to her more tightly. "What did she do? Leave everything to charity?"

Oh, dear, Helen thought, surely Eleanora hadn't bequeathed her millions to Save the River? If Floyd Baskin was getting it all, she'd eat her party hat.

"It won't go to a charity, ma'am," the sheriff said and cleared his throat. "It's going to Lady Godiva. Looks like Eleanora left the whole kit and caboodle to the cat."

Chapter 23

HELEN INSISTED ON riding back to Eleanora's house in the sheriff's car with Zelma. Jean had decided against going back to Eleanora's—"I wouldn't feel right," she'd told Helen, "not until Biddle's got this thing solved"— and Lady Godiva would be escorted home by the attorney after the party was over.

As they pulled up in front of the Victorian mansion, Helen gazed up at the pillared veranda with a sigh, wondering if it was Lady Godiva's house now. How did a cat pay bills? Or hire someone to mow the lawn? She still couldn't get over the fact that Eleanora would leave her assets to a feline.

Helen loved Amber dearly, but she couldn't imagine bequeathing her estate to him.

Once they got inside, Zelma said she was feeling better but excused herself to use the restroom. Helen attacked the cupboards in the kitchen, scrounging up tea bags, cups, and saucers.

"It's not quite like it sounds," Biddle explained from his seat at the kitchen table. "The lawyers tell me everything's set up on a bunch of conditions. It pretty much goes like this." He cleared his throat. "As long as Lady Godiva's being cared for, Zelma can stay in the house just like always. She'll get a salary to keep up the place, much as she did when old Mrs. Duncan was alive and kicking."

"So Stanley doesn't inherit a penny?" Helen asked.

"Not a red cent."

"I still can't believe it," Helen said as she filled the teakettle and put it on the stove to boil. "I just can't believe she'd do this to Zelma. The poor dear has given her life to Eleanora and her family. It doesn't seem fair, does it?"

For once, Biddle appeared at a loss for words. He met her eyes, shaking his head. "No, ma'am," he said, "it doesn't."

Oh, Eleanora! Helen couldn't help thinking. How could you have done this to Zelma, and her so devoted? Helen could only imagine how devastated Zelma must be, how crushed to find that her Miss Nora placed a cat in higher esteem than a whole life of service.

The teakettle whistled, the shrill noise cutting through Helen's thoughts. She quickly pushed them aside, fixing up three cups of Earl Grey.

She added a sugar bowl and spoons to a tray and carried it over to the table, handing one cup to Biddle and setting the others out for herself and for Zelma, though the housekeeper had still not reappeared.

Helen sighed, settling into a chair across from the sheriff and warming her hands on the teacup. "So where does that leave you?" she asked, looking up. "As far as the investigation goes, I mean?"

Biddle toyed with his tea, stirring in a heaping spoonful of sugar, the steam rising like a veil before his face. "I think it leaves me where I started. So far as I'm aware, no one but the lawyers knew about the terms of Eleanor's will. So money's still a motive and, of course, good old-fashioned hate." He looked Helen straight in the eye. "Both seem to support a case against Jean Duncan."

She stared at him. "You can't mean it?"

"I do."

Helen squared her shoulders and glared at him. "I don't believe it," she told him, "and neither will a jury of her peers."

He raised a hand to quiet her. "Consider the facts," he said.

"The facts as you see them," Helen murmured and pushed aside her tea, feeling the strain of this morning— and of the days before it—wearing her patience paper-thin.

"Think about the evidence," Biddle went on, rising to his feet. He stepped away from the table and paced around it, slapping one hand on the other for emphasis. "It pointed to her from the beginning. My gut told me she did it. If you think about it, everything fits." He paused across from her and planted his palms on the table, the resolution plain in his face. "Her fingerprints were on the container of pâté."

"As were Zelma's prints," Helen reminded him, "and Eleanora's."

"Jean admitted to putting the containers in the refrigerator. She had Splat in her kitchen at home. No one would've been the wiser if things had gone according to plan, if Zelma hadn't panicked when Eleanora was having spasms and come after me."

She had certainly panicked, Helen thought, remembering how agitated Eleanora's housekeeper had been the night she'd shown up at the diner. She'd been positively broken up. It was such a stark contrast to her subdued reaction when the sheriff had divulged that Lady Godiva was the beneficiary of Eleanora's assets.

Zelma had acted like a zombie, not saying a word during the drive from town hall in Biddle's car. Compared to her histrionics at Eleanora's "goodbye party"—for want of a better description—Zelma had taken the news about the will stoically. It was almost as if she'd already known.

"Ma'am?"

She glanced up to find the sheriff watching her. He'd tugged his hat on his head and looked ready to go.

"I asked if you'd like a ride home."

Helen couldn't leave Zelma just yet. "No, I'll stay a bit," she told him.

He seemed relieved when she turned him down.

"I am sorry how things turned out," he apologized, "but I'm just doing my job."

Helen imagined that was what Judas told himself, but she bit her tongue. She sat at the table with the teacup in her hands, feeling completely ineffectual as Biddle shrugged and headed out of the house. He was probably on his way to arrest Jean.

Good heavens.

She grabbed her phone out of her purse and dialed Jean's number, cursing under her breath when she only got voice mail.

Where was Jean? Surely she couldn't still be at town hall?

Helen left a message—"The sheriff's not budging, I'm afraid, so you might want to get a lawyer on the horn"—then she hung up, realizing there was little Jean could do beyond that except to stay out of Biddle's reach for a while. It wasn't as if she could run off to Brazil.

Helen tried to convince herself that everything would work out, that it would be all right. She had always been so convincing when she'd said it to her kids and grandkids. So why didn't she believe it now?

She thought of going home and reading a book or doing a crossword puzzle, anything to take her mind off this befuddling case.

But first she needed to find Zelma, who seemed to have disappeared since their arrival back at the Duncan house. Had she decided to lie down?

She went left from the hallway out of the kitchen, passing a laundry room and finding the door to the housekeeper's room half opened. The bed was neatly made, the bureau top devoid of objects, and the floor perfectly swept. The attached bathroom was small but tidy.

It was as though no one really lived there.

On a whim, Helen tugged at the top dresser drawer, pulling it toward her.

It was empty.

She pushed it closed and opened the second drawer, then the third after that. All were bare save for the faded floral liner at the bottom.

Her heart thudding, she checked the small closet. A dozen wire hangers littered the floor. There were no shoes, no suitcase stored above. Nothing.

Had Zelma cleared her things out even before the party? Had she been planning to take off before Biddle even found whoever had killed Eleanora?

Helen stared at her own puzzled reflection in the mirror, and something hit her.

Oh, no. No, that couldn't be right.

Thoughts began to race through her brain, connecting bits and pieces that she hadn't been able to string together until that very moment.

Jean's fingerprints were the only ones found on the container besides Eleanora's and Zelma's. But Zelma had told the sheriff Jean had put away the food herself.

The housekeeper had taken the news about Eleanora's will without expression, as though it had come as no great shock. Had she known about Eleanora's plans to leave her estate to the cat?

"Oh, Zelma," Helen whispered to the mirror, frowning

at herself. Was it possible? Had she been so intent on root-
ing out Eleanora's enemies that she'd overlooked someone
very, very close?

There was only one way to find out.

Helen stepped out into the hallway and began to walk.
"Zelma?" she called out as she hurried through each of the
rooms downstairs, not finding the housekeeper in any one
of them.

Despite feeling worn down by the past few days, Helen
made herself trudge up the stairs and peered into each of
the bedrooms. But still there was no sign of the missing
housekeeper. Up to the third floor she went, doing the
same as before, having no luck there either. By the time
she'd explored all the rooms, her clothes felt sticky against
her skin. She wiped a sleeve against her damp brow, wondering where on earth Zelma could be.

Helen hadn't heard a car start. Even still, she headed
downstairs to check the garage. Beside an older-model
Mercedes that had once belonged to Marvin, there was
a brown four-door sedan that Helen realized must belong
to Zelma.

She went up to the car and peered through the windows.

Lo and behold, a small suitcase lay on the backseat
with a smaller tote bag set in the well. Helen leaned her
head against the glass, feeling defeated.

Could Zelma truly have killed her mistress? Why else
would she be packed and ready to run?

Helen backed away from the dark brown Ford but

stopped at the sight of the grill. Before her eyes flashed an image of the car that nearly ran Eleanora down.

Could it have been Zelma?

Miss Nora hired me when I was just sixteen.

Zelma had never married, had never had a life of her own apart from the one Eleanora Duncan had given her. She'd devoted herself to Eleanora's family. Had she grown to resent her mistress after so much time? Especially when she'd learned that Eleanora had left her nothing but her regular salary so long as she cared for Lady Godiva? Zelma had given up everything for Eleanora, and Eleanora had given her so little in return.

So money's still a motive and, of course, good old-fashioned hate.

Biddle's words returned to haunt her.

And Helen realized that he might just be right after all.

"Zelma!" Helen tried again once she was back inside the house. Finally she opened the door to the basement, the one place she hadn't looked.

Helen detected a dim light filtering from a basement room below the sharp descent of wooden steps. She stood at the top of the stairs for a moment, listening, certain that she'd heard movement.

"Zelma! It's Helen Evans," she called out and started down. "I just want to know that you're okay."

The steps creaked relentlessly beneath her feet as she went down into the unfinished space. Heavy beams and ductwork passed over her head as she made her way toward the glow of light, ending up in a big room with a bare bulb dangling from above. Metal shelves piled high with tools and boxes filled the walls. Sheet-draped furniture had been pushed into the nooks and crannies.

"Zelma, is that you?" she asked, warily approaching another doorway. She was sure she heard shuffling feet and someone grunting. And it sounded like liquid being sloshed around. Helen's first thought was that Zelma was mopping.

Until she inhaled the pungent odor of gasoline.

When she peered into the room, her eyes widened.

"Good God, what's going on?"

For an instant, the face turned toward her. Light glinted off the thick, round glasses. Tufts of hair in disarray framed anguished features. The blue polyester dress Zelma had worn to town hall was smeared with dirt and dust.

"You shouldn't be down here," Zelma said. "You shouldn't have come."

Helen stood where she was, too surprised to do much of anything except watch, suddenly understanding what Zelma was up to.

Wooden shelves lining the walls were filled with old cans of paint and thinners. Stacks of twine-bound newspapers littered the concrete floor, along with old blankets and rags, everything damp from the gasoline Zelma had emptied atop them from the nozzle of a rusty-looking container.

"Zelma, don't do this," Helen found her voice to plead. "You'll make everything worse."

"It can't get any worse!" the housekeeper shouted and tossed the empty gas can at Helen. It clattered on the concrete floor, landing inches from her feet. "Go away and leave me be," Zelma cried, fumbling in the pockets of her dress. "This is my mess, not yours."

"You killed her, didn't you?" Helen said, and the smell of the gasoline filled her nose, making her head hurt. "You put the poison in Jean's pâté, knowing she'd be blamed if it came down to it. Everyone in River Bend knew of the feud between them. No one in their right mind would've suspected you, not the woman who'd cared for Eleanora all these years, who'd given her life to the Duncans."

"You couldn't begin to understand," Zelma shouted back. "You have no idea how I felt. How I feel."

"You saw her will, didn't you? Had she changed it recently?"

Zelma hesitated, hands crammed in her pockets. Her shoulders shook as she said, "Miss Nora kept the papers lying around on her desk for a week, long enough for me to read every last word. She even had me deliver them to her lawyers." Her voice quivered unmercifully. "I nearly tore them up and threw them out."

Helen wondered how it had come down to this. How could Eleanora have placed so little value on the one person who'd never left her side? "No, you didn't destroy Eleanora's will. You poisoned her instead."

"I don't want to talk about it! It's over and done, and I can't change what happened!" With trembling fingers, Zelma drew a pack of matches from her pocket, nearly dropping them before she got them open.

Helen couldn't believe the woman really meant to burn the house down. Her blood pounded in her head so that she could hardly hear her own voice. "Miss Nora let you down, I know, but I can't honestly believe you hate her so much to burn this house—"

"Hate her?" Zelma's red-splotched face turned toward Helen. The light danced off her glasses so that she looked like a woman gone mad. "I never hated Miss Nora! I loved her with all my heart. It was that stupid cat I hated. I meant to put the Splat in the cat food, but I put it in the wrong container." Tears swam down her cheeks. "If only the cat had died, Miss Nora would have needed me again. But my eyes are so bad I mixed things up!"

"You made a mistake," Helen said, and something bubbled up in her chest; relief, perhaps, at not having been so wrong about Zelma after all. She could well understand Zelma mixing up the gourmet cat food for the pâté in the container marked The Catery.

"Now the cat's going to have what should be mine?" Zelma struck a match and held it up. "No," she said, "I don't think so. It isn't right. It's just not right."

A lump of fear filled Helen's throat as she watched Zelma lower her arm. "No!" she cried out, about to lunge forward.

But Zelma dropped the burning stick to the gas-soaked heap at her feet. With a pop, the combustible pile exploded.

Helen fell backward.

Flames rose into a solid wall of fire, crackling and snapping as they leapt higher and wider. Smoke quickly filled the room, choking off Helen's breath.

"Zelma!" Helen found enough air in her lungs to scream, her heart racing as the smoke and flames spread between them. The heat pushed Helen back toward the stairs and away from the fire and Zelma.

Chapter 24

HELEN COUGHED CONVULSIVELY, drawing her hand to her face, her breaths choked off as the fire sucked the oxygen from the air.

She backed up until she bumped into the wall. Then she felt her way through the smoky haze. Her eyes burned, and her throat felt hot and raw. Adrenaline coursed through her veins. She had to get out of there and fast. She couldn't risk trying to help Zelma. She only prayed there was some other way out and Zelma could escape. The flames were everywhere, feeding on the paint cans and storage boxes that filled Eleanora's basement.

Helen blindly made her way up the stairwell, holding onto the railing. Her lungs aching, she hacked with every breath.

She dashed up the steps and burst free of the basement, closing the door behind her as she gasped for fresh air. Even still the smoke followed her, seeping beneath the door and swirling about her feet like the fog in an old movie.

Without another thought, she snatched Eleanora's phone from the wall and dialed 911. The moment the voice asked, "What's your emergency," Helen blurted out, "There's a fire in the basement of the Duncan house on Harbor Drive in River Bend! The woman who set it might be trapped down there. Please, hurry!"

As smoke began to fill the kitchen, Helen ran to the back door and pushed her way out to the driveway. As she made her way free of the house, coughing and sputtering, she felt thankful that Lady Godiva wasn't inside.

She fell to her knees on the grass, shrieking as an explosion shattered the glass in the front windows. Helen buried her head in her arms, afraid to look up until she heard the sound of a fire engine approach.

As she pulled herself up from the lawn, she saw that curious neighbors had begun to gather on the driveway. Helen walked toward them, glancing back at the house to see blue-tinged flames licking at the broken windows.

The noise of sirens grew loud in her ears, and she spotted the engine from Grafton turning from the street onto the drive. It honked its horn as it drew closer to the Duncan house. Men in protective gear hopped off as soon as the vehicle stopped. Calling out to each other, they unleashed a never-ending hose from the top of the truck and hooked it to a nearby fire hydrant.

The hundred-year-old house crackled and groaned as the fire bloomed. The flames reached as high as the gingerbread-latticework atop the porch. Helen winced every time another window popped and shattered.

"Oh, Zelma," Helen murmured, as the crowd around her thickened and the cacophony of voices and noises from man and machine nearly deafened her.

Someone reached for her then, calling her name, and she found Sheriff Biddle holding onto her arm, his face so near her own that his nose touched the tip of her nose.

"What the hell happened?" he yelled.

"Zelma," she cried in return. "She killed Eleanora, but it was a mistake!"

"What?" He pointed to his ear. He couldn't hear her.

Helen shook her head in frustration, leaning in closer and shouting, "Zelma lit a fire in the basement. She didn't come out with me!"

His frown deepened, and she knew he'd understood her every word.

A fireman came their way, gesturing at them and the other onlookers, warning them to back off, urging them away until they stood on the sidewalk.

From there Helen watched as the men fought the flames. The way the firefighters held the hose looked like a tug-of-war. Helen couldn't tell at first who was winning: them or the fire. Her eyes filled with tears at the thought of Zelma inside, and she clasped her hands at her breasts, praying silently, knowing she'd just have to wait it out.

It was two hours before the fire was brought under control, though it was another hour still before the crowd of spectators disbanded, along with a van from the *Alton Telegraph*.

As the firemen hosed down the still-hot embers, Helen repeated her story to the fire captain and then again to the sheriff.

"She admitted she killed old Mrs. Duncan?" Biddle asked as though he didn't believe her.

"Yes." Helen nodded. Every breath she took still felt tinged with smoke. "She didn't mean to kill Eleanora. Lady Godiva was her intended victim. She thought that if she got rid of the cat, Miss Nora would shower her with affection. Only she mistook the cat food for the pâté from The Catery." Helen squinted at the remains of the once grand house. "Can you imagine devoting yourself to someone for sixty years of your life and then watching them treat a cat better than they treated you?"

"She confessed all of this?" the sheriff said, still seemingly unconvinced that Helen hadn't made it all up to save her friend.

Helen turned on him then, rage shaking through her and rattling her voice as she replied, "I'm not lying, Sheriff! Zelma said as much herself! She had her bags packed. I saw them in the back of her car! She planned to set the place on fire then take off for heaven knows where."

"This is nuts," Biddle remarked and pushed his hat

back on his head, wiping at his sweat-damp brow. "I can't believe it."

"But it's true, every word." Helen swallowed down the grit in her mouth. "Do you think I could make something like that up?"

The sheriff cocked his head and looked at her like he was trying to figure that out.

Helen wanted to kick him.

"Sheriff?"

A fireman with a soot-stained face approached. "We think we found the woman you said might still be in the house."

"Is she alive?" Biddle asked, but the expression on the fellow's face made Helen's heart sink.

"I'm sorry," the fireman said. "It looks like she tried to get out through the cellar doors around back. She was on the stairwell. It was the smoke that got to her, not the fire," he explained, though it comforted Helen little.

"She didn't deserve that," Helen murmured. "She may have been wrong, but she didn't deserve to die."

Biddle said nothing.

"Again, I'm sorry," the man remarked before he walked away, and Helen hugged herself, trying to stop the trembling.

"Well, it's over at least," the sheriff said.

Helen nodded as she stared at the remains of the house. The once lovely Victorian mansion that had outlived uncountable floods was scorched and blackened by flames.

It looked weary, with its gaping windows and splintered wood; defeated.

As Helen thought of Eleanora and Zelma, her heart felt near to breaking.

"Yes, it's over," she whispered, "but it's not a very happy ending."

"C'mon," Biddle said, putting a hand on her shoulder. "I'll take you home."

For once, Helen didn't fight him.

Chapter 25

HELEN PLUCKED OFF her bifocals and put aside the crossword from that morning's paper.

She couldn't seem to concentrate on the puzzle, no matter how hard she tried. Her mind kept going back to what had happened to Zelma Burdine.

Sighing deeply, she stared out through the porch screens. Though she gazed upon trees and bluffs, on the bridge that spanned the nearby creek, Helen didn't see the beauty in her surroundings. She could only think of one thing: Zelma had poisoned Eleanora.

Helen couldn't help feeling sorry for Zelma despite everything. How it must have hurt to realize she was prized far less than a four-legged pet.

"Helen?"

She glanced at the door to see a woman standing beyond the mesh. She squinted and quickly realized who it was. "Come on in, Jean," she said, forcing a smile and waving a hand. "The door's open."

Jean Duncan stepped inside, dropping the door closed with a clatter.

Her silver hair was tied back in a brilliant red scarf, and she looked peaceful in a way Helen hadn't seen since before Eleanora's murder. "I hope I'm not interrupting."

"Nonsense." Helen cleared away a half-read book and the newspaper so she could make room for Jean on the wicker sofa.

Her friend sat down beside her.

"It's good to see you," Helen said and reached over to give Jean's hand a squeeze.

"I can't thank you enough," Jean told her, and she suddenly looked anything but serene. Her hazel eyes seemed on the verge of tears. "I don't know what I would've done without you this past week. If it hadn't been for you, Biddle would've had me locked up in the Jersey County jail."

Helen felt her skin warm. She squirmed and picked some of Amber's pale fur off her sweatpants. "I knew you were innocent," she said, "and the sheriff surely would have figured it out before long, even if I hadn't poked my nose where it didn't belong."

Jean fiddled with the gold chains at her throat. "Well, just the same, I'm glad I had you on my side. If I'd depended on Sheriff Biddle to get to the truth, it might've been a long wait."

"Now, Jean, he was just doing his job," Helen said, repeating words told to her not so long ago, in fact. And she hadn't liked them then any more than Jean appeared to now.

Her friend let out a slow breath. "I'm awfully happy to be off the hook, but it's terrible the way it all turned out, isn't it? Poor Zelma," Jean added in a whisper, and her eyes filled with tears. "It might be a good thing that she didn't have to live with the guilt of accidentally killing someone she loved. It's heart-breaking."

"Oh, Jean, what happened with Jim was an accident," Helen said and took her friend's hand. "If only Eleanora had been kinder to you and Zelma both. Sometimes grief just gets the best of us."

Jean shook her head. "I just wish it had all turned out differently."

"Well, what's done is done." Helen tried to cheer her friend up. "You need to look ahead now and put the past behind you."

Jean glanced down at her lap. "If only I could," she said. "But I have a feeling my catering business is over before it's begun."

Helen smiled. "I talked to Verna Mabry myself, and she's willing to hire you to cater the annual luncheon. So I'd imagine you'll need to get started on the menu. You do know how picky the LCIL ladies are."

Jean looked up, and this time the tears in her eyes were anything but sad. "Yes," she said, "I guess I do."

"Just stay away from goose liver pâté, all right?"

"Oh, I will," Jean laughed. "I definitely will."

AT NOONTIME, HELEN headed for the kitchen to make herself a sandwich. She nearly tripped over Amber en route.

He flew ahead as if determined to beat her in a foot race. Then he promptly sat down at his empty saucer. While Helen opened up a fresh can of cat food, she eyed the floor around her hungry feline, noting that all the ants had completely disappeared.

She found herself thinking that Splat really did the job—maybe too well in some cases.

Leaving Amber in the kitchen devouring Ocean Whitefish 'n' Shrimp, Helen took her sandwich to the porch. She heard the crunch of tires on gravel and looked up to see Frank Biddle's black-and-white pulling up just before she could take a bite of grilled cheese.

He slammed the car door and hiked up his trousers as he walked up her stone path. The porch steps creaked when he climbed them. He doffed his hat, smoothing his palm over his head before he raised a fist to knock.

"Mrs. Evans? Is that you?"

"If it's not," she said, "will you go away?"

He grunted and opened the door despite the lack of invitation.

"Ma'am," he murmured and took a seat opposite her at the table, the wicker crackling as he settled in and plunked down his hat. His eyes seemed to jump from one end of the porch to the other, touching upon everything but her.

"Is there something I can do for you?" she asked him.

"Well, Mrs. Evans, it's like this," he started, though

she had a feeling she was going to have to drag whatever it was out of him. "I have a couple things I need to tell you."

She settled back in her chair and waited.

He shifted in his seat. "First off, Jemima Winthrop took in old Mrs. Duncan's cat. Though I guess she's a Duncan now, too, isn't she?"

Helen stared at him. "Jemima has Lady Godiva? How does that affect the will?"

"I don't know exactly," he told her and openly eyed the gooey sandwich on her plate. "My guess is they'll try to get something out of caring for the critter."

Helen sniffed. "Well, if they don't come out of this a few dollars richer, it won't be for lack of trying."

"Guess we'll just have to wait and see where the dust settles, won't we? That is, once the estate goes through probate."

Helen picked up half of the grilled cheese, only to put it back down. She pushed the plate away, not having much of an appetite.

"You gonna eat that?" Biddle asked.

Helen smiled. "Are you hungry, Sheriff?"

"A little," he said and reached across the table. He picked up half the sandwich and took a big bite, muttering with his mouth full, "They're settling down here, by the way."

Helen blinked. "Jemima and Stanley?"

"Yep," he got out as he swallowed. "She said they'll live in the old Winthrop place. Stanley claims he's gonna fix her up."

"It could surely use some fixing."

Biddle took another bite, chewed thoughtfully, and nodded. "Oh, and you were right about something else."

Helen's ears pricked up at that, and she noticed the sheriff's ears turn red as did his cheeks.

"It appears Miss Burdine was planning on running away. The garage wasn't too badly damaged, and we recovered her bags from the Ford. She took a few things that weren't hers though." He licked grease from his fingers before ticking off on them, "A sapphire necklace, a pair of diamond earrings, an ivory brooch, and a couple of platinum rings."

"Oh, dear," Helen said and thought again how much she hated unhappy endings.

She heard the pitter-patter of paws on linoleum and glanced over as Amber made his grand entrance. His yellow eyes first fixed on her and then on Sheriff Biddle. Not at all impressed by the company, he turned his tail and sashayed over to a sunny spot at the opposite end of the porch.

"It's sad," she remarked, "how blind we are sometimes to what's right in front of us." As Eleanora had overlooked Zelma, she was thinking, but Biddle obviously took her words to mean something else.

He wiped his hands on his pants and got to his feet, hooking his thumbs in his gun belt. "Uh, ma'am, I wanted to . . . well, I figured that maybe I owed you . . . " His voice trailed off, and he cleared his throat.

Helen looked up at him, waiting.

"I realize I gave you a hard time about interfering in

the investigation," he said and shifted on his feet. His face flushed upward from his collar. "But I really, um, figure I should offer you—"

"My grilled cheese," she cut him off with a smile, holding out her plate. "If you want the rest, it's yours."

Susan McBride's (Mostly) Healthy Tomato-Pesto Grilled Cheese

You'll need:

> Two slices of a hearty whole-grain bread
> One beefsteak or Roma tomato
> Several slices of smoked mozzarella cheese
> Pesto
> Mayonnaise (preferably vegan)
> Spread or butter

Set a skillet to medium heat. If desired, use olive oil or spray to keep sandwich from sticking.

Prepare two slices of bread by generously smearing one with pesto and the other with vegan mayonnaise. Cut two slices of beefsteak tomato (or more if you use a Roma tomato) and lay on top of the pesto. Cut two or three slices of smoked mozzarella (or smoked Gouda if you prefer). Place on top of the tomato and put your sandwich together. Before placing in skillet, smear spread or butter on top side of bread, then carefully flip sandwich so that butter-side is down in the skillet.

While the sandwich is grilling, coat the top side of bread with butter or spread so that it's ready when you need to flip it. Let the sandwich get nice and golden brown on each side so the cheese melts.

Carefully remove from the skillet and enjoy!

Read on for a sneak peek at

SAY YES TO THE DEATH

the new mystery in Susan McBride's
USA Today bestselling
Debutante Dropout series!

Prologue

MILLICENT DRAPER YAWNED and nudged her owl-like glasses back up the bridge of her nose, leaving a smudge of ivory fondant on the tortoiseshell frames. Her plastic-gloved fingers were smeared with the stuff. Her knuckles felt stiff, and she could barely keep her eyes open. She'd worked through the night on a wedding cake for Senator Ryan's daughter, Penny, and she hadn't slept a wink. Olivia La Belle, the bride's wedding planner, had phoned at six o'clock the night before—just as Millie was closing up shop—and demanded an early delivery. "Sorry, Millie, but the ceremony's been pushed up a wee bit," Olivia had said in a honey-sweet twang that implied softness when Olivia was anything but.

Four whole months was "a wee bit?" Millie thought with a groan.

"We need the cake by three o'clock tomorrow sharp," Olivia had insisted, her sugared drawl turning hard. "The ceremony's at five with a sit-down dinner reception to follow. If you don't get this done, it will make me very unhappy. Do you understand what I'm sayin', darlin'?"

Oh, yeah, *darlin'*, Millie understood. Ticking off Big D's premier event planner was a big no-no. Olivia might as well have said, "If you don't get this done, you're as good as dead in this town."

Ever since Olivia had done weddings for an Oscar winner and the spawn of a former president her head had blown up as big as Texas. She'd become society's go-to-girl, and not only for Dallas royalty but honest-to-God foreign royalty and Hollywood's A-list. She'd even fina-gled her own reality TV show on a cheesy cable network and used it to promote herself and to punish those who displeased her. Anyone who dared defy the Wedding Belle risked hanging a "going out of business" sign on the front door.

Millie had seen it happen most recently to her dear friend Jasper Pippin, a floral designer in Big D for decades. Fed up with Olivia's lies and demands, he'd finally drawn a line in the sand. "She lied her tight little ass off and said the tulips I had flown in from Amsterdam for the may-or's wife's birthday party were half-dead," Jasper had told Millie, moaning. "She threatened a drubbing on her TV show if I didn't eat the cost. I'm going to lose my shirt if she keeps pulling these dirty tricks."

"What will you do?" Millie had asked him.

Jasper had drawn in a deep breath and said, "I'm going to let her have it."

So the always civil Jasper had finally squared his thin

shoulders and stood up to Olivia, sure that other vendors who'd been jerked around would follow suit. Only no one dared, and Olivia had blacklisted him. His orders had begun to dry up one by one until Jasper had to shutter his doors, claiming early retirement though Millie knew better.

That evil woman had her French-manicured fingers in so many pies around Dallas that everyone who worked with her was scared to death. Even Olivia's own assistant seemed skittish, and with good reason since the job seemed to involve a revolving door. The gangly college grad, Terra, who followed her everywhere taking notes on her iPad never seemed to say anything but "Yes, Olivia" and "Of course, Olivia," like a well-trained parrot.

Millie wished she'd had the gumption to tell Olivia that she could take this impossible cake deadline and stuff it, but she couldn't risk losing everything she'd worked so hard for. She'd started Millie's Cakes in her own kitchen thirty-five years ago and had built her impressive client list from scratch. She wasn't ready to give it all up because she'd ticked off the very fickle Ms. La Belle. Unlike Jasper, she had no intention of being forced into early retirement.

Millie swallowed, glancing at the clock on the wall. With a noisy *tick-tick*, its hands crept toward seven.

She had only seven hours left, and she still had to attach the two hundred handmade sugar orchids she'd painted a delicate shade of purple. Her feet ached from standing, and her arthritis was acting up so that her fingers felt like unbendable sticks. If the shop wasn't so busy, she would have turned the whole shebang over to her staff but they had other orders to fill, cakes that had been on the docket for months and were equally important.

No, this monkey was squarely on Millie's back.

If she blew this job for Senator Ryan's daughter, it would be on her head, no one else's. She tried to convince herself that she couldn't blame the bumped-up time frame entirely on Olivia. That silly Penelope Ryan was the one at fault.

"Damned girl got herself knocked up," Millie muttered, having heard the gossip that the bride's belly had begun to pop and that the senator—a button-down conservative if ever there was one—wanted his daughter legally wed ASAP. He couldn't afford to have the nineteen-year-old college sophomore he'd painted as pure as the driven snow during his campaign get photographed walking down the aisle in a maternity gown.

"You can put her in a big white dress and marry her off but that doesn't change anything," Millie murmured and pushed at her glasses again.

Was the senator going to pull one of those "the baby came prematurely" routines when his grandchild popped out in another five months or so? People didn't seem to have a whole lot of sense these days, but most of them could count so long as they had enough fingers and toes.

Ah, well, Millie mused, there would always be brides who got knocked up before their vows. There would always be disappointed fathers who wanted to pretend their darling daughters stayed virginal until their honeymoons. And there would always be bitches like Olivia La

Belle behind the scenes, wielding a phone in one hand and cracking a whip with the other, either telling everyone off or telling them what to do.

Millie sighed.

"Enjoy your moment while it lasts, Queen Olivia," she whispered, thinking of Marie Antoinette and her date with the guillotine. "As for me, I will let them eat cake," she added, knowing that Olivia would get her comeuppance one of these days. Women like her always did. Millie just hoped she'd be around when it happened. Heck, she'd pay good money for a front row seat.

But for now Millie blinked her bleary eyes and tried to keep her hand from shaking as she delicately affixed the edible orchids to the seven layered concoction she'd created overnight.

She would get this damned cake done or die trying.

Chapter 1

"IF WE'RE TOO LATE, we'll get stuck in back and we won't be able to see a thing," Cissy complained as she drove with one manicured hand on the wheel and the other madly gesticulating. "For heaven's sake, Andrea, how long does it take to brush your hair and put on a dress?"

"Longer than the five minutes you gave me," I replied, wondering how I'd gotten roped into this cockamamie date with my mother when she had a perfectly good fiancé who could have escorted her to the bumped-up wedding of a Texas senator's spoiled daughter. I had a perfectly good fiancé of my own who was sitting back at my condo, a beer in his hand, watching the Stars take on the Blues in the Stanley Cup play-offs, which sounded a whole lot better than what I was doing at the moment.

"Steven couldn't come," my mother said as though reading my mind—something she did far too often, and it freaked me out every time. "He's off to Augusta for a golf outing with some old IRS cronies."

"You mean he didn't dump his plans for you even though he'd rather be in his yoga pants watching a hockey game with Malone?" I threw out for good measure.

"His yoga pants," my mother sputtered, "watching a hockey game with Brian?" Her brow tried hard to wrinkle. Then she blinked and gave me a sideways glance. "You're talking about yourself, aren't you?"

"Of course, I'm talking about myself," I growled, tempted to ask if Botox killed brain cells, but I refrained.

My mother sighed and did a very odd thing.

"You're right, I'm sorry, sweetie. I shouldn't have gotten huffy. I really am glad you could come to my rescue at the last minute," she drawled and reached over to pat my thigh. "You're a very good girl, and I appreciate that you're tagging along with me."

I opened my mouth but nothing emerged. Yes, I, Andrea Blevins Kendrick—smart ass extraordinaire— found myself speechless. My mother didn't often offer apologies, unsolicited or otherwise.

"Truly, I didn't intend to drag you out on such short notice but I only got the call from Shelby Ryan just before I went to bed last night. I had no idea they were moving up Penny's wedding to today," my mother explained. "It was too late for Steven to back out of his golf weekend, and I didn't want to pressure him."

No, I thought. No use making Steven feel bad when it was all too easy to guilt me into going instead.

"What about Sandy?" I asked referring to my mother's Girl Friday. Sandy Beck had been Cissy's personal assistant for as long as I could remember. She'd had as much a hand in raising me as my mother and couldn't have been more a part of our family if she'd been blood. "Why isn't she your date?"

"She's visiting her sister in Magnolia, Arkansas, and won't be back 'til next Sunday," Mother told me with a sigh. "Honestly, I tried."

"It's all right," I murmured and added, "I can survive a few hours away from my yoga pants and Malone." *Two hours tops*, I told myself. That was all. Then my dress would turn into rags, my coach into a pumpkin, and I'd be all the happier for it.

Although I wasn't sure I would survive wearing Spanx. I could already feel them strangling my intestines. Unfortunately for me, my mother didn't consider jeans and T-shirt proper attire for a swanky wedding; unfortunately for Cissy, my closet was full of jeans and T-shirts and little else. I did have one little black dress that I'd kept around for a decade in case of emergencies; but Cissy had nixed it the moment I'd offered. "Who wears black to a wedding?" she'd remarked with a sniff. "Morticia Addams?"

Instead my mother had deemed herself my fairy godstylist, bringing over a new pair of Spanx along with a fresh-off-the-rack-at-Saks Carolina Herrera springy floral dress that was made for skinny women who survived on lettuce and water and/or had the meat sucked off their bones in seasonal liposuction sessions. It would have probably involved amputation or a bottle of Wesson oil to get me into the thing without the gut-strangling Lycra underpants. So for my mother's sake—and, boy, was she gonna owe me big-time—I wriggled into the killer girdle and the über snug dress though I could barely breathe let alone eat a piece of wedding cake without rupturing an organ.

"Why was the wedding moved up?" I dared to ask, something Mother hadn't yet explained although I had a pretty good idea. When I'd last heard Cissy mention the invitation to Penny Ryan's knot-tying, it was set for late summer. It was now the middle of April. There was only one reason I could fathom for such last minute maneuvering. I muttered, "The word 'shotgun' comes to mind."

Cissy sighed. "Well, I'm not one to gossip."

I laughed and replied, "Since when?"

My mother's Rouge Coco lips settled into a disappointed moue. She tossed her coiffed blond head and drawled, "Well, that was hardly very nice. I'm sure they taught you better in your Little Miss Manners classes all those years ago, or I should ask for a refund."

"Oh, for crud's sake," I said under my breath and rolled my eyes. There wasn't a Highland Park matron who loved to gossip more than Cissy Blevins Kendricks, the Doyenne of Beverly Drive, and every socialite within a ten-mile radius knew it.

"So how far along is the bride?" I asked point-blank.

"About four months as near as anyone can tell," Cissy blurted out, and a spark lit her eyes. "Shelby said Penny's starting to show, which is why they had to do the wedding stat. In another month, she wouldn't fit in her dress."

Ha! I thought with a smirk, so much for detesting gossip.

"Shelby said the latest scan showed that the baby's a boy," my mother rattled on, hardly able to stop herself. "They're all pleased as punch since Penny's an only child. She promised to name the boy after Daddy Vern." Cissy took her eyes off the road long enough to turn her head and give me a wicked smile. "Vernon Ignatius Tripplehorn," she said, adding, "Quite a mouthful isn't it? They want to call him Iggy."

"The poor kid," I muttered. "That'll virtually guarantee a regular ass-whooping by junior high if not sooner."

And I should know. Being nicknamed "Andy" by my father early on—though my mother had always insisted on calling me Andrea—meant I'd heard plenty of playground cracks about being a girl with a boy's name.

"Well, Penny might not have gone about things the proper way but at least she's giving Shelby a grandchild," my mother went on, and I saw her squint behind her oversized sunglasses, peering at the signage overhead as she drove south toward Preston Hollow. "Some of us are still waiting," she said with a sideways glance before gliding toward the toll road exit.

Oh, joy, I thought, *here we go again.*

At least my mother was progressing in a forward direction when it came to guilt trips. Ever since Malone and I had gotten engaged the year before, she'd begun dropping less than subtle hints about wanting to become a grandmother. "Don't wait too long," she'd said most recently, "or that womb with a view will start looking like Miss Havisham's cobweb-filled row house." Somehow, the digs about my ticking clock were easier to take than the jibes that came before Malone had put a ring on my finger. For years, my mother would lay it on thick when she wanted me to do something for her, reminding me of how I'd broken her heart by refusing to debut when I was eighteen shortly after my dad had dropped dead from a heart attack. My big ol' white deb dress that Mother kept hanging in my old bedroom closet as a constant reminder of what I'd "missed" would surely have had cobwebs on it by now save for the fact that my mother had a maid tasked with banishing cobwebs from the house.

And, yes, I knew I'd wounded her deeply for being a debutante dropout. Since my conception, she'd envision my following in her footsteps: coming out to society, pledging Pi Phi at SMU, marrying a bona fide blue blood, and settling down in Highland Park. But I hadn't done any of those things. I wasn't Cissy. Wearing a white dress and kidskin gloves at cotillion had been *her* dream for me, not mine. Losing my father had made me realize that life was too short to live someone else's dream for them. So despite how hard my mother had tried to draw me back to the dark side, I'd fought just as hard to become my own person, whether she liked it or not.

Heck, I was still fighting.

". . . and they had to throw off the media so he's letting them use the place since it's been sitting on the market for months anyway," I heard Cissy saying as I shook off my thoughts and realized we'd somehow landed on Alva Court with its ginormous mansions tucked safely behind guard houses and privacy fences.

"What?" I said since I'd obviously missed the most important part of her monologue. "Who let them borrow their place for the wedding?"

"Lester Dickens," Cissy announced and gave me a "for goodness' sakes" look when I appeared genuinely puzzled. "The oilman," she told me as if that explained everything. "He's got his house on the market since he split with his fourth wife. The court ordered him to sell and split the profits with Fifi or Phoebe, whatever her name is. Les told Vern and Shelby they could use it for Penny's big day since no one's livin' in it at the moment. His soon-to-be-ex is at their condo in Vail, and Vern's been staying in a suite at the Mansion."

The Mansion being The Mansion on Turtle Creek, of course, one of Dallas's swankier hotels. It was a go-to spot for the very rich when they wanted to run away from home but not *too* far.

Click.

A light bulb went on in my brain, and I put two and two together. Lester Dickens was Senator Ryan's biggest supporter and had put together a PAC and bought TV ads out the wazoo to help good ol' Vernon get elected in the first place. It was no wonder Dickens had loaned his buddy his mansion for a day. He was probably even more anxious than the senator to get the pregnant Penny married off.

"It's actually a good thing you came with me, sweet pea. It'll give us some ideas for *your* wedding," my mother nattered on as she pulled her Lexus up to a pair of gates, rolling down her window to give her name to a security guard. "Your old classmate from Hockaday, Olivia La Belle, will be here. Shelby hired her for Penny." Cissy drawled as the guard stepped back and the gates parted before us, revealing a sprawling Mediterranean villa sitting at the end of a very long driveway beyond palm trees and cascading fountains.

"Did you say Olivia La Belle?" I repeated because I hadn't heard anything else my mother had said after the name. And all of a sudden I was flashing back to prep school and the athletic blonde who used to taunt me during Phys Ed. *You must be a boy, Andy Kendricks, 'cause you have no boobs at all! Andy's a boy, Andy's a boy!*

I flinched as though I'd been hit hard with one of Olivia's carefully aimed dodge balls, and I rubbed my arms. I could still feel the bruises.

"Yes, Olivia La Belle," mother repeated and wrinkled her nose. "Do you have wax in your ears, sugar plum?"

My mouth was too dry to tell her my ears weren't the problem.

"I thought we'd chat her up and see if she's available any time soon," Cissy said, clearly ignoring the stricken look on my face. She steered the Lexus past a long line of shiny Caddies, Mercedes, Range Rovers, and Beamers that took up one side of the driveway and some of the expansive front yard. She finally turned into the circle around the fountain and pulled up to the valet. "You and Brian really need to firm up the date. Wouldn't it be the bee's knees, havin' your old schoolmate in charge of your wedding?"

Was Cissy insane?

La Belle from Hell planning my wedding?

I shuddered at the thought.

"Absolutely not," I said, plain and simple, and gave my mother the evil eye as we got out of the car; but she ignored me, smiling at the valet as she handed over her keys. Hiring Olivia wouldn't be the bee's knees at all. It'd be more like being swarmed by an entire, very angry beehive.

About the Author

SUSAN MALLERY is the *New York Times* bestselling author of the Fool's Gold romance series, as well as *Three Sisters*, *Barefoot Season*, *Already Home* and *Chasing Perfect*. She lives the writer's life in sunny Seattle with her husband and her tiny but intrepid yorkie.